The Trouble with Dreams

Lee Ann Lewis

HERALD PRESS
Scottdale, Pennsylvania
Waterloo, Ontario

Library of Congress Cataloging-in-Publication Data
Lewis, Lee Ann, 1954–
The trouble with dreams.
p. cm.
Summary: Joseph's ability to interpret dreams causes him many problems before proving to be a gift from God.
ISBN 0-8361-3571-7 (alk. paper)
1. Joseph (Son of Jacob)—Juvenile fiction. 2. Bible. O.T.—History of Biblical events—Juvenile fiction. [1. Joseph (Son of Jacob)—Fiction 2. Bible. O.T.—History of Biblical events—Fiction.] I. Title.
PZ7.L58724Tr 1991
[Fic]—dc20 91-27503
CIP
AC

The paper used in this publication is recycled and meets the minimum requirements of American National Standard for Information Sciences—Permanence of Paper for Printed Library Materials, ANSI Z39.48-1984.

Library of Congress Catalog Number: 91-27503
International Standard Book Number: 0-8361-3571-7
Printed in the United States of America
Book design by Paula M. Johnson/Cover art by Joy Dunn

1 2 3 4 5 6 7 8 9 10 97 96 95 94 93 92 91

The Trouble with Dreams

Lee Ann Lewis

For Mama Jewel,
my grandmother.
Your energy, your love,
and your walk with the Lord
have inspired me all of my life.

1

JOSEPH was awake long before the sun came up. There was no sound outside his tent, for everyone else was still sleeping. Soon his father, Jacob, would wake up and build the morning fire. Soon Leah would begin cooking breakfast. But now it was quiet, and Joseph lay on his bed thinking.

Today his ten older brothers would be leaving to take the flocks of sheep to a pasture far away. They did this every spring. When they arrived at this pasture, three of the brothers would stay there with the sheep for two months. The rest of the boys would return home in a few days.

Joseph was twelve years old, and his father had never let him go on this outing before. It didn't seem fair! Most of the other brothers had been allowed to go when they turned ten. Joseph wanted to go with them so badly he could taste it! Somehow he must find a way to go. He *had* to convince his father he was ready to join the other brothers.

Waiting for just the right moment to talk to his father wasn't easy. Jacob was busy this morning, trying to get everything ready for his sons' trip. Food had to be packed, the flock had to be checked, and there were a hundred last-minute instructions for Reuben, the oldest son. Joseph grew nervous as the time to leave approached. Finally he saw his father sit down beside the fire for a short rest. It was now or never.

"Father, there's something I need to say to you," Joseph tried to make his voice sound manly. "I think they could use some more help on their trip. The flock is bigger than last year, and I'm afraid they might run into trouble. They need an extra pair of eyes and ears." Joseph waited for Jacob's reply. His voice might have sounded casual, but his heart was beating wildly!

Jacob had been absently working a knot out of two strips of leather. Sighing, he put the leather down and turned his attention to this new problem. "Joseph, we've been through all this before. I need you around here while they're gone. There will be plenty of time for you to go later. Now please, I've got a lot to do." With that, Jacob stood and started to walk off.

"I'm almost thirteen. Everybody around here treats me like a baby! You let Reuben go when he was only ten. It's not fair!"

Jacob turned. He faced Joseph eye to eye. For a minute, both were silent. When Jacob did finally speak, his voice was surprisingly soft and kind. "Oh, Joseph. What am I going to do with you?" He sighed. He suddenly seemed old and tired.

To his young, impatient son, the answer was taking forever. Finally Jacob spoke again. "You're right. I haven't been fair. I'm just afraid something might happen to you, and I don't know what I'd do then."

"Nothing is going to happen. I'll be fine. I'll do everything Reuben tells me to do, I promise! Please let me go!" Joseph gazed into his father's eyes, because Jacob always respected someone who looked him in the eye.

Another minute passed before Jacob said anything. "I've let my own fears get in the way of your growing up. Yes, you may go. But I'll remember your promise to obey Reuben. And I probably won't get any sleep until you're back safe. Now you'd better hurry. They're almost ready to leave," Jacob smiled and left Joseph standing alone.

Joseph wasted no time getting his things together. He rolled his heavy tunic, his bow, and two arrows up in his bed blanket. He put his knife in its sheath around his waist. In minutes he had joined his ten older brothers and his father.

"Where is *he* going?" It was Simeon, the next to oldest brother. It was obvious by the look on everyone's face that Joseph wasn't exactly a welcome addition to the trip. When Jacob declared that Joseph was allowed to go, eyes rolled. Sighs and groans came from everywhere.

"He is going. That's final. Reuben, you are responsible for him, and he has promised to do what you tell him," said Jacob sternly.

"Alright. Joseph, you're in charge of the donkey. Keep up with him; he's carrying our food, water, and blankets," Reuben wasted no time barking out his first order.

Walking beside a donkey! Anybody could do that. Joseph was so disappointed. How was he supposed to prove he was a man with a stupid job like that? Well, he would just make the best of it. Joseph knew better than to argue with Reuben before they had even left!

Jacob had words of instruction and blessing for each of the eleven sons. Only six-year-old Benjamin would remain at home. To Joseph, Jacob simply said, "I am remembering your promise." Then they bowed for prayer together in the soft light of that early morning.

Joseph's brothers had left on dozens of journeys before, and each time Jacob had prayed for their safe return. But this time there was added anxiety in his voice. Joseph knew it was because he was joining his brothers for the first time. *No matter what happens,* thought Joseph, *I will make him proud of me.*

Jacob stood beside his youngest son, Benjamin, and watched eleven young men, one donkey, and a large flock of sheep disappear beyond the hilltop. No one could know how much his heart ached at letting Joseph go.

2

JOSEPH could hardly believe he was really off on this journey. He had never been away from his father before and felt very grown-up. He planned to savor every minute of this new adventure. He took a deep breath. It smelled like fresh green grass and sheep. What a day!

Because Joseph had never taken the sheep before, he was eager to learn all he could. He already knew the reason for moving sheep from one pasture to another. Sheep graze constantly and can literally pull up grass by the roots. With as many sheep as Jacob had, it was amazing how quickly they could destroy a pasture. Unless they were moved often, there would be nothing left of the fields. Taking them to another place for a while gave the grass time to grow again. But moving flocks as large as these took skill.

He watched his older brothers work. The many sheep had to be constantly counted to make sure none strayed. Each brother was responsible for a certain number of sheep, and within each of these groups of sheep there was one dark-colored sheep. This was the "marker." A quick count of the markers would tell Reuben that all the sheep were accounted for.

Besides keeping up with the number, it was important to keep the sheep calm. Any sudden noise or movement and the whole flock might panic and scatter all over the hillside. To keep this from happening, the brothers hummed soft tunes to the animals. Occasionally someone whistled to a lamb that was wandering, but other than that no one spoke.

They walked for hours. By afternoon, the sun was high overhead, and it was getting hot. Unfortunately, the calming tunes intended for the sheep had the same effect on Joseph. He began to get sleepy. The sound of his donkey's sharp hoofs on the stony ground was the only thing that kept him awake. He was tired and bored and hungry. But no one else was complaining, so Joseph didn't either.

Finally they reached a well which had belonged to their grandfather, Isaac. Simeon said, "We'd better stop here for the night. It will take two hours to water all the sheep, and by then our daylight will be gone." Those were the sweetest words Joseph had heard all day!

By the time the sheep had been watered and a fire had been built, Joseph was exhausted. His face was sweaty and dirty. His feet ached. He drew cool water from the well and splashed it over himself.

When he returned to the fire, Joseph was delighted to see that his brothers, Gad and Dan, had killed five rabbits with silent arrows that afternoon. The rabbits, split in half, were roasting over the fire and giving off a delicious aroma. Joseph's mouth watered and his stomach growled.

"I'm starved! When do we eat?" he said.

"*We* don't," Reuben's voice was icy. "Didn't we mention that the youngest of the group always has to provide his own rabbit? Why do you think Zebulun wanted you to come along so badly?" This remark was met with laughter and agreement from the other brothers.

Joseph didn't think it was a bit funny. It was true that Zebulun was just older than Joseph, but it seemed unlikely that he was ever subjected to this "rule."

Joseph knew the real reason behind their unfair treatment. All the brothers resented Joseph's special place in their father's heart. Joseph's mother was not Leah. His mother, Rachel, had died when Benjamin was born, and Jacob had grieved for her ever since. Because of this, Jacob favored Joseph and Benjamin openly, as if loving them more would somehow bring Rachel back.

Sometimes this made Joseph uncomfortable, but he loved his father so much that he said nothing. And now he was miles away from his father, so his brothers were free to take out their resentment on him.

Joseph poked at the fire with a stick and fought back tears of humiliation and homesickness. This was not the adventure he had hoped for. And he had never had to go without supper. He watched his brothers carefully remove the sizzling rabbits from the fire. They carried on lively conversations while they ate with their mouths full. They not only ate the meat, but noisily sucked on the bones, removing every morsel.

Joseph's stomach was so empty it began to hurt. But he was determined to behave like a man. He would obey Reuben, no matter what. Tomorrow he would kill his own rabbit.

But what if I don't even see one? he thought to himself. *What if I shoot at one and miss? What if I do kill one? I'll bet Reuben wouldn't even let me roast it over "his" fire!* The thought of raw rabbit made Joseph sick to his stomach. When he finally went to sleep that night, he dreamed he was herding a huge flock . . . of rabbits!

The next morning all the brothers were up while it was still dark. They ate dried figs and bread for breakfast. To Joseph's empty stomach, it tasted like a wonderful feast.

Just like the day before, everyone walked without speaking. As before, the sheep bleated, the brothers hummed, and the donkey wheezed and snorted in Joseph's ear.

But Joseph was not the same as the day before. Today he carried his bow and arrows across his back. Today he would be ready. Today he was watching. Every large stone, every small shrub, every clump of grass might be hiding tonight's supper. By noon he had a pounding headache from straining his eyes in search of a rabbit.

They stopped to rest for a few minutes under a grove of trees. Drinking water from a bag slung over the donkey's back, they discussed the direction of the far pastures.

"We need to head straight over that range of low hills." Simeon had been on this journey many times, and knew the safest route. "It should only take about another day or so."

Levi and Asher had another idea. "By turning toward the east, we could save time. Those low hills are tough on the sheep."

"They may be tough on the sheep, but Father has wells along that route. If we go east, we have no wells!" Reuben explained patiently. "The sheep can't go without water tonight."

"Ah, but there is a well to the east," said Levi. "It belongs to a man named Asben. I'm sure he wouldn't mind if we used his water."

"Especially if we don't tell him," laughed Asher.

Glaring at Joseph, Reuben said, "What if someone told Father?"

Levi looked at Joseph too, then smiled. "I don't think anyone will."

3

JOSEPH had never been to the far pastures before, yet he seemed to know that his brothers were not going the right direction. All their talk about using a man's well without his permission made Joseph uneasy. He watched his brothers closely as they herded the sheep. They were uneasy, too. They kept scanning the hillsides nervously. They were looking for any signs that would show that Asben might be in the area.

At one point, Reuben quietly sent Levi off over an adjacent slope. Joseph wondered why. He would have asked Reuben, but just at that moment, a rabbit darted from behind some tall grass!

The donkey, startled by the quick movement, bolted from Joseph's grasp. There was no time to worry about the donkey now. The rabbit ran toward a cedar thicket, with Joseph close behind. He reached for an arrow and held it loosely against the bow string.

Now he must keep a close watch on the rabbit, or he

would lose sight of it in the thicket. Scampering behind a small rock, the rabbit stopped dead. Joseph stood frozen in place, ready to aim and fire. The occasional twitching of the rabbit's long ears was the only clue to its whereabouts.

Unfortunately, Joseph couldn't see anything but those ears. He would have to wait for a better shot. Patience. He was breathing heavily from excitement. Would the rabbit never move?

Yes! First one little hop, then another. The little rabbit cautiously ventured out from behind the rock. Patience . . . just a few more seconds. Slowly, Joseph pulled the bow back and took a deep, steadying breath. The rabbit's ears twitched once more. In another second it hopped forward into the clearing.

Aim for the shoulder, keep it steady. Swishshsh! The arrow flew from his bow, and found its mark. The rabbit was dead.

"Yippeee!" yelled Joseph. "Supper tonight!" He ran down to where the rabbit lay and carefully removed the arrow. After wiping the blood from the tip, he replaced it in his quiver.

Taking his knife from its sheath, Joseph jerked the limp rabbit up by its back feet and quickly split its middle. His hands were much practiced at this task, and in a moment the rabbit was gutted and skinned.

Joseph cleaned off his knife, and wrapped the rabbit carcass in the loose end of his tunic. He would wet the tunic with water from the bag when he reached the donkey. At least he wouldn't go hungry tonight!

The afternoon sun sent long shadows slanting from the shrubs and rocks. When Joseph finally reached the top of the slope, he was out of breath, and his head was pounding from the heat. His brothers had herded the sheep down toward a dry ravine and they seemed to be miles away.

But what discouraged Joseph most was the absence of the donkey. He scanned the flock again and again, but there was no sign of the stupid animal. Joseph finally remembered that the donkey had bolted when the rabbit ran out of the grass. Now it was gone, and Joseph was responsible. If he ran to catch up with his brothers, he might never find the donkey, and they would be furious with him. But if he spent too much time looking for his long-eared friend, he might lose sight of the flock entirely.

The thought of being lost on the countryside alone sent a wave of panic through him, and he started to run. He was almost crying again. This had to be the worst two days of his life! Was this what being a man felt like? If so, why was he still acting like a little boy? Joseph was so busy being mad at himself he almost missed seeing a familiar sight.

There on the ground off to his right was a small blanket. It belonged to his brother Dan. The donkey had probably thrown it off while still running scared. There might be others, too. Maybe the stupid animal wasn't so stupid after all. Joseph picked up the blanket and trotted off on the mysterious trail of the donkey.

He lost all track of time. The sun dropped lower and lower. It occurred to Joseph that before long it would be too dark to see anything, much less a blanket hidden in tall grass. He slowed to a walk, and counted up all his miseries. He was alone. He was lost. The donkey was gone. Now his brothers would have no blankets or food for the night. He had made a mess of things.

Joseph stopped walking and sat on a big flat rock. The tears he had held back for two days finally fell, all at once. There was no one to hear him now, but Joseph wouldn't have cared if there had been. All he wanted was to be back in his tent with his father. "Wouldn't he be proud of me now?" Joseph said out loud.

He sat on the rock and watched the colors of the sunset. He tried to think how his father would handle this problem. What would he do first? Joseph knew the answer to that. His father would pray.

So Joseph slipped down off of the rock and got down on his knees. Placing his elbows on the smooth, warm rock, he closed his eyes and sighed.

"Lord, how did I get into such a mess?" Joseph's voice was still hoarse from sobbing. "I only wanted to prove that I could be grown-up, too. I wanted my brothers to love me. I wanted to be one of them. Now they'll hate me even more." He began to cry again.

"Please God. Help me! Help me find the donkey. Get me back home safely. I promise I'll do better next time. . . ." Joseph was silent for a few minutes. He didn't know what else to say, so he just said "Amen."

He walked on in the twilight, hoping to find a spring before it got completely dark. He was so thirsty and dirty. Dried rabbit's blood was still on his hands, and he was sticky with sweat. And if he didn't stop and build a fire soon the rabbit would be too spoiled to eat.

He had just about given up finding water when he heard the wonderful splashing noise of a tiny spring. It took him several minutes to find it among the tall grass, but when he did, he fell flat on his stomach and drank the water as it bubbled out of the ground.

Night found Joseph dozing by a small blaze. He had cleaned the rabbit's bones of all traces of meat. With his belly full and his body washed by cool spring water, Joseph drifted into a deep, exhausted sleep. It would be his last good night of sleep for several days.

4

THE grass rustled softly. Joseph was still asleep. In his sleep, he heard noises, but it took several minutes for the noises to wake him. Finally he opened his eyes—and found himself staring directly into the wheezing nose of his own donkey! The animal had seen the fire and wandered to the source of its light. Joseph was so happy that he jumped up and threw his arms around the donkey's neck.

Most of the blankets were gone, and the water bag had a huge hole in it, but the bread and dried fruit were still there, and at least the animal was back. Suddenly Joseph remembered his prayer from the night before. God really had heard it. Not only that, God had answered it, too! "Thank you, Lord, for finding the donkey, and for helping me through last night." It was a quick prayer, but Joseph wanted to thank God for being with him.

In minutes, Joseph and the donkey were on their way. Now all they had to do was find the rest of

Joseph's family. The morning was cloudy and refreshingly cooler. Inspired by finding the donkey, Joseph walked quickly and steadily toward the north. He knew he had worked his way eastward last night and figured he would eventually meet up with the flock somewhere in the foothills. Stopping only for a quick bite of bread, Joseph continued until late afternoon.

He listened occasionally for sounds that might lead him in the right direction, but the countryside was quiet. The longer he walked, the more worried he became. He fought the panic that kept building inside.

Just as he was giving way to despair again, he reached the top of a hill and met a welcome sight. There in the next valley was the entire flock, grazing peacefully! His brothers had just finished watering the last sheep. Joseph yelled and took off. He raced down the slope, with the donkey trotting to keep up. The brothers' faces registered their surprise; they had not expected to see Joseph again anytime soon, much less the donkey.

"Where have you been?" roared Reuben. "Do you realize we almost froze last night—and had to go without breakfast because of you?" He was furious, just as Joseph knew he would be.

Reuben continued his rebuke. "We can't build a fire tonight. There is too much danger of its being seen. Had you not returned with the food, we would have had nothing to eat at all!"

No one seemed glad to see him. No one was relieved that he was alright. All they cared about was the food. Joseph was hurt by their stinging remarks. He was blamed for the hole in the water bag, too.

That night everyone was cross. Trying to ease the tension, Joseph asked Zebulun who Asben was. "He's a Canaanite, and he has not exactly offered us warm words of welcome."

"Hopefully he'll not know we've been here until we're long gone." Those casual words were not matched by any confidence in Reuben's voice. "Now I suggest we get some sleep. I plan to be miles from this well by daylight."

True to his words, they were far away before Asben ever knew they had been there. The next full day's walking brought them to their father's far pastures. There they set up a small camp that would serve as home for Levi, Judah, and Issachar for the next two months. These three brothers would stay there with the flock until the end of the summer. It was a short distance to the nearby village where additional supplies could be obtained.

That night, long after dark, the four oldest brothers left the camp and walked toward the village. Joseph saw them leave but was sleeping soundly when they returned at daylight. They were cross, tired, and mostly silent, but Joseph gathered that whatever they had gone into the village to do had been worth the walk.

In another two days, eight of Jacob's sons had returned to their father's home. The journey was reported to be a success. Reuben did not tell Jacob about Joseph losing the donkey and getting lost. At first Joseph was relieved to be spared this embarrassment. Then he began to realize why his older brothers were silent. They expected silence from Joseph in return.

Joseph tried to act pleased about the trip in front of his father, but inside his heart was burning with shame. He had never held a secret from his father before. Jacob often looked into Joseph's eyes, and seemed to see right through him. Jacob knew something was bothering this young boy, but he would wait until Joseph wanted to talk.

Finally one night, long after the supper fire had died away, Joseph went to his father's tent. "I've been waiting for you," said Jacob.

Joseph went inside and told his father everything. He told him about the rabbit, and about losing the donkey. He told about his prayer and God's answer. He told about Asben's well, and about his brothers' mysterious trip into the village.

It was as if a great weight had been lifted from his shoulders. Joseph slept peacefully that night for the first time in many days. But he could not have known that his words of confession to Jacob were overheard by one of the brothers.

Their anger burned silently at Joseph. He had betrayed them, and they would never forget. Never.

5

IT had been a harsh winter. Jacob's family struggled to keep their flocks alive and to stay warm and healthy themselves. But finally the winter ended, as all seasons do. Now it was springtime.

Four years had passed since Joseph, now seventeen, first went with his brothers to the far pastures. During those four years, Joseph had spent more and more time taking care of the sheep with his brothers. He had learned how to be a good shepherd.

Jacob was proud of Joseph. He was pleased to see his son grow into such a handsome young man. Joseph was tall and strong. His dark, wavy hair reminded Jacob of beautiful Rachel. If only she could see her oldest son now!

Perhaps it was Joseph's likeness to Rachel that made Jacob give him extra love and attention. His brothers resented this, but Joseph didn't seem to notice. He loved his brothers, as well as his father. He worked hard, and enjoyed this happy time in his life.

Springtime was Joseph's favorite time of the year. He liked the way the air smelled, and he liked to see green grass slowly cover the dry ground on the hillsides.

"I think the days are warm enough now," said Jacob one evening after supper. "We have a big job to do. The flocks are larger than ever before."

"Why do the sheep have to be sheared, Father?" asked Benjamin. "Couldn't they just wear their heavy coats in the summer? It only grows back by fall anyway."

"Nice try, Benjamin. You're just trying to get out of helping with the shearing," Levi's eyes twinkled as he spoke to his youngest brother.

"Benjamin, we shear the sheep for two reasons. First, just imagine if you had to wear that wool coat in the summer heat!" Jacob had ignored Levi's accusations and was patiently answering Benjamin's question.

"But the main reason we shear the sheep is so we can use the wool ourselves. We use it to make our own clothes, then we sell what is left to buy other things we need to survive. That's why it's so important that everyone pitch in to help."

Benjamin's weak effort to get out of work had not paid off. He sighed and stood to go to bed. "I just wish there was an easier way to get that wool off," he mumbled.

Shearing flocks as large as Jacob's took several days. Joseph and his brothers wrestled with the frightened sheep, who often kicked with razor-sharp hooves. One at a time, the sheep were herded into a tiny pen. The skilled hands of the older brothers quickly shaved thick, dirty wool, starting just below the sheep's head.

Once the wool was finally removed, the sheep was released to romp and play on the hillside, happy to be rid of the extra weight. To Joseph, a lamb without its woolly coat looked like a silly long-legged rat. This amusing change of appearance always took a bit of getting used to.

Each sheep produced enough wool to fill a whole basket. After Leah and her maids washed the wool on the rocks in the river, they stretched it out to dry in the sun. Later they would pull and stretch the wool, wash it some more, then pull and stretch it again. When they were finally finished, the wool was ready to be spun and woven. Jacob came to Leah at the end of this hard week of work.

"Leah, I want you to find me the whitest wool our sheep produced. I have something special in mind; I will need the best of this year's shearing."

Jacob knew that Leah always watched for a sheep that was especially white. When that sheep was taken to be sheared, she made sure its clean wool would not be mixed in with dirty wool from other sheep. This clean, white wool was what Jacob now wanted.

Leah didn't question why Jacob wanted the wool. Instead, she went quickly to her tent and brought out a heavy cloth bundle. She proudly opened it to show off what was inside. "Will this be white enough for you, Jacob?"

Taking the soft, milky white wool in his hands, Jacob smiled. "Perfect! It is even better than I hoped!" His approval made Leah blush. After being married to

Jacob for so many years, she still loved to make him happy.

Jacob carefully wrapped the wool back in the cloth. "Leah, one more thing. This is to be a surprise. Please don't tell anyone that I have asked for this special wool. Do you understand?" Although his voice was stern, Jacob's eyes twinkled with excitement.

Leah nodded. Jacob returned to his tent with his prized possession.

The next day, Jacob announced at breakfast that he would be leaving for a few days. Benjamin asked, "Where are you going, Father? May I come with you?"

Too often, Benjamin was left at the camp with Leah. She usually put him to work grinding meal or hauling water, and he hated those boring jobs.

"No, Benjamin. This time I must go alone. You need to stay and be of help around here." Jacob noticed the disappointment on his youngest son's face. He smiled, "I will be back in a few days. Perhaps I will bring you something special."

In an hour Jacob was ready to leave. Joseph noticed that his father carried a large cloth bundle under the folds of his tunic. Joseph wanted to ask him what it was. He wanted to ask where he was going. He wanted to know why his father was acting like he had a secret.

But Jacob wasn't telling anyone anything. Offering a prayer for blessings and safe travel, he left. It would be five long days before his return.

6

It was Joseph's turn to take the newly sheared sheep up to the hillside pasture. After lunch, he gathered the things he would need: his knife, some bread and dried meat for supper, and a small blanket for the night.

"Benjamin, why don't you come along with me? I could use an extra pair of eyes and ears." Joseph knew how much his little brother hated being left at home.

"Thanks, Joseph! I've never been up to the hillside without Father! This should be great fun. I'll take my bow in case there are wild animals."

Benjamin's excitement reminded Joseph of his own eagerness to join his brothers for the first time. This was memory touched with pain. Joseph thought of the things that had gone wrong during that trip. Since their return, his brothers had never really welcomed Joseph as one of them. They remained cool and distant, and at times even hostile. Benjamin was the only real friend Joseph had.

"Joseph, Benjamin tells me you want to take him with you up the hillside." It was Leah's voice. She didn't sound pleased. "I'm sorry, but he can't go. I have work for him to do around here."

"Leah, surely there are others who could help. Please let him go, he's so disappointed Father has left him here."

"I know. But his chores at home are more important than a romp up the mountainside. You'll have to go alone. I won't discuss it further!" The firmness in her voice let Joseph know her mind was made up.

Sadly, he told Benjamin the bad news. "Don't worry, Benjamin. One day soon I'll take you with me."

It took Joseph about two hours to guide the slow animals up the slope to the hillside pasture. He was hot and tired. Under the shade of an old cedar tree, Joseph relaxed to watch the flock. There was not much to do. The sheep knew the pasture and seemed content to graze quietly. Although he didn't intend to, Joseph soon let his mind wander. Before he knew it, he had fallen fast asleep.

The breeze blew softly around his head, and he began to dream. At first, the dream was blurry and confusing, as many dreams are. But gradually the picture in his mind grew clearer. In the picture there was a beautiful summer sky. The wind blew gently over a field of grain. Joseph and his brothers were working. They were binding the grain into sheaves.

As the dream continued, somehow the people in the picture disappeared. Only the sheaves of grain were left lying in the field. Suddenly Joseph's sheaf rose and stood proud and tall. The sheaves of his brothers gathered around Joseph's sheaf and bowed down to it. At once, Joseph awoke from this strange dream.

"They were bowing down to me!" Joseph spoke aloud, still amazed at the picture lingering in his mind. He had a puzzled frown on his face and was lost in thought.

Then slowly the thought came to him: might the dream he just had come from God? As he pondered this, his excitement grew. Joseph stood and turned his face toward the sky. "You have given this dream to show me what is to come. But God, I don't understand. What does my dream mean?"

It was quiet. There was no answer. Not yet. But somehow Joseph knew that eventually God would reveal the meaning behind the dream. He looked once more on the flock of sheep. They were grazing and bleating quietly as if nothing had happened! Didn't they know that he had just been part of a miracle? Didn't they care?

The rest of that day and night Joseph watched over the sheep, but his mind was far away. He was thinking about the dream. When would the answer come?

The next day he returned home. With his father still away, Benjamin was the only person who seemed glad to have Joseph back. The rest of his brothers had little to say, as usual. Joseph longed to share his dream.

As the family sat around the fire after supper, Joseph could no longer keep quiet. He waited until there was a break in the conversation.

"Something strange happened to me on the hillside yesterday." He tried to sound casual, but there was excitement in his voice.

"Let me guess," said Levi. "You managed to lose the entire flock of Father's best sheep!" This remark drew sneers and laughter from the other brothers. Only Benjamin remained genuinely interested.

"Tell us what happened, Joseph!" His eyes were wide. He was hoping a pack of wolves had tried to attack the flock, only to be courageously fought off by the heroic Joseph!

Ignoring the ugly laughter of his older brothers, Joseph said, "I fell asleep. . . ." But before he could continue, Asher interrupted him.

"You fell asleep. Well, that *is* strange! I suppose for the past seventeen years you've been wide awake!" The others broke into more laughter and sarcastic remarks. Joseph was embarrassed and angry. Would his brothers never take him seriously? Well, perhaps they would when they found out what he had dreamed!

"If you'll just let me finish. I fell asleep and had an incredible dream. We were all out binding sheaves of grain, when suddenly my sheaf stood upright.

"Then *your* sheaves—" Joseph paused for a dramatic effect, "your sheaves gathered around mine and bowed down to it!"

At first they were silent. Then someone laughed. Now they all laughed, a loud, hateful laugh.

Simeon finally spoke. "So, little brother, you actually intend to reign over us? Oh mighty ruler!"

He stood and bowed his head. "Forgive me. I had no idea I was in the presence of a king!" He threw back his head and roared with laughter.

The others also stood and pretended to bow before him. As they left the fire to go to their own tents, their laughter rang through the still night air.

Only Benjamin was left. He asked Joseph to explain the dream, but Joseph didn't answer. He was too shocked and humiliated. The dream was so real. It was so important. He knew God would bring the dream to life. Then his brothers would see. They really would bow down to him . . . someday.

7

JUST as the noon meal was finished, Jacob returned, exactly five days after he had left. He seemed weary from his long walk, but he was happy to see his family. He asked questions about the flock. He wanted to know if anything important had happened while he was gone. No one mentioned the dream.

"Father, what is that large bundle you have with you? It's even larger than the one you had when you left." Benjamin was always curious. But this time his father offered no answers.

"Never mind, Benjamin, it is something private. But if you will look inside my cloak, you will find that I have brought back some sugarcane for you."

Jacob's gift satisfied Benjamin. He forgot all about the bundle.

Late in the afternoon, when the older boys were busy with chores, Jacob called for Joseph. The two went inside Jacob's tent. It was hot and bright outside, but inside the tent the sand felt cool beneath Joseph's feet. Joseph had to wait a minute or two for his eyes to adjust to the indoors.

Then he saw it. Laying out upon the mat where Jacob slept was a heavy wool coat. Its beauty made Joseph gasp. He slowly walked over to the mat to examine the coat more closely, for it was like nothing he had ever seen.

Several strips of wool had been dyed a deep purple. Still other strips were a bright scarlet. These colored strips were woven tightly into a pattern that ran the entire length of the coat. Jacob gently lifted the coat and held it up to Joseph's shoulders. Its sleeves came to Joseph's fingertips, and the bottom of the coat brushed the top of his sandals.

"Try it on! Try it on!" Jacob could barely contain his excitement. He was like a child showing off a new toy. He held the heavy coat while Joseph, bewildered, put his arms into the long sleeves. It was a perfect fit.

"Father, it's beautiful! But I don't understand. Where did it come from? Why are you giving it to me?"

This time when Jacob spoke, there were tears in his eyes. "Joseph, you are the oldest son of my beloved wife, Rachel. She has been dead for many years, yet I still grieve for her every day.

"I see so much of her in you. You are wise, and honest. You understand things your older brothers never will. This coat is my gift to you for being the son so close to my heart. Wear it always. It will remind both of us of our love for each other."

Although it had not been spoken, they both understood that this coat was more than just a gift. It was a symbol. A symbol of the blessing and birthright that

Jacob wanted to one day give to Joseph.

That night, Joseph proudly wore the coat for the first time before his brothers. They could not believe what they were seeing! Here was their brother, whom they hated anyway, wearing this—this *kingly* robe. They shrank from their memory of the dream in which their sheaves bowed before Joseph's.

As Joseph strutted around the camp, their bitterness grew. Would there be no end to this parade of boasting and pride? The long sleeves and sweeping length told still another story. No one could possibly do any real work in that garment. Now Joseph would not have to do his share of the chores. They couldn't stand the sight of him, or that coat! Each of the brothers went to bed that night nursing fierce resentment.

Joseph, on the other hand, carefully removed the coat and went to bed thanking God for this wonderful gift.

The night winds blew gently outside the tent. Joseph was dreaming again. This time he was surrounded by a night sky. As he stood in the middle of this sky, the sun, moon, and eleven stars bowed down to him.

It was a powerful and moving dream. When Joseph awoke the next morning, he was anxious to share it with his family.

At breakfast, he appeared in his colorful new coat. Jacob smiled proudly, but the others only glared at him. As they ate their silent meal, Joseph casually mentioned that he had had another unusual dream.

Jacob, who had not heard about the first dream, was interested. "Tell us what it was, son."

Joseph explained the details of his dream. As he

mentioned the eleven stars, Joseph pointedly looked at each of his brothers. The meaning of this look was clear to everyone!

"What are you trying to say, Joseph?" Jacob's voice held surprise and shock. "Do you mean that your mother and I and your brothers will actually come and bow down to the ground before you?"

The laughter and sneers from his brothers on hearing the first dream were nothing compared to the rebuke in Jacob's voice now. Joseph felt his face grow hot with embarrassment. How he wished he had never told anyone about those dreams! Now even his father was angry.

What did it all mean? Joseph had been so sure that the dreams had come from God, yet they seemed to cause nothing but trouble. Just how much trouble they would land him in, Joseph was about to find out.

8

"JOSEPH, I am worried about your brothers," Jacob spoke softly. "I just can't rest until I know that everything is alright."

The older boys had taken a large flock of sheep to graze near Shechem. They had been gone almost a month and Jacob was uneasy. Not too long ago these same sons had gotten into a fight with the men of Shechem. Now, two years later, they were grazing their sheep there. Would they be alright? Or would there be more trouble? Jacob had to know.

"Why don't you let me go to Shechem and find them? I can make sure that all is going well, then I will come back and tell you. It should only take a few days to catch up with them. They're probably wondering how things are going here, too," Joseph spoke to Jacob as reassuringly as he could.

"Thank you, Joseph. When you have sons of your own someday, you will understand that a father always wants to know that his sons are safe."

Leah, too, was happy that Joseph would be going to Shechem. Most of Joseph's brothers were Leah's sons, and she was anxious to hear how they were doing. She prepared an elaborate meal for Joseph to take with him. She baked loaves of barley cakes loaded with dried figs. She wrapped soft goat cheese in a damp cloth, and packed strips of salty dried goats meat.

The meal was heavy for Joseph to carry, but he knew how much it meant to Leah. This was her gesture of love for her sons. Besides, Joseph looked forward to sharing the meal with his brothers.

Shortly after breakfast, Joseph put on his coat, bowed for prayer with Jacob, and left for Shechem. He walked for three long days, but the weather was cool and Joseph enjoyed being out on his own. He arrived at Shechem just before nightfall. It was too late to try and find his brothers, so he spent the night near the village well.

The next morning, he was wakened by the sound of bells. The villagers were taking tiny herds of goats, each one wearing a bell around its neck, to nearby pastures. Joseph was anxious to find his brothers, so he quickly washed his face with cold well water and headed for the nearby fields. But the brothers were nowhere to be found.

By lunchtime, Joseph had wandered up and down every hillside pasture in the area. He was exhausted and frustrated. Where on earth could they be? What if something terrible had happened? He was determined to keep searching, even if he had to walk all night.

As he came to the top of a hill, Joseph spotted an old man sitting alone under the shade of a tree. The man had apparently been watching Joseph from a distance.

"Young man, what are you looking for? You've been wandering around these fields all day!" The old man's voice was shrill, but his eyes were kind. "Have you lost a sheep? Wouldn't be surprised if a wolf hasn't found it by now!"

"No," said Joseph. "I haven't lost just one sheep. I've lost a whole flock, and ten brothers, too! They were supposed to be near Shechem, but I haven't seen any sign of them. I'm afraid something terrible has happened."

"Ten brothers? Well, don't worry. They're alright. I saw them myself just three days ago. They had been grazing around here for a long time. I guess they figured there were greener pastures somewhere else."

Those words were like cool water poured over Joseph's troubled mind. "Where did they go? Did you hear them say where they were going?" Joseph's heart was beating fast. He was so close, yet what if the man didn't know? Without any direction, Joseph might never find them.

"Sure I heard them. They were heading for Dothan. That's just another fifteen miles from here," the old man smiled and spit through his rotting teeth. "You ought to be able to catch up with them by morning."

Joseph thanked the man, and gave him a loaf of Leah's barley-fig bread. Then he started for Dothan. The man had said they were alright. Joseph could have just returned to his father with that good news. But he knew that Jacob would want to hear from the brothers themselves. Besides, he couldn't face Leah without telling her how everyone had enjoyed the meal!

Joseph walked the rest of the afternoon and evening. By nightfall, he was just too tired to go any further. He built a tiny fire beside a stream, and sampled some of Leah's good food. Tomorrow he would find them. Tomorrow they would be happy to see him. Tomorrow. . . .

9

WITHIN an hour after he started walking again the next morning, Joseph heard the sweet familiar sound of bleating sheep. He was just coming over the gradual crest of a field when he spotted his father's flock in the valley below. The brothers were resting under a tree a long distance from where Joseph was.

He thought they saw him, so he raised his arms high and waved. One of the brothers, he couldn't tell which, waved back. It would take him another half hour to finally reach them. He was so anxious to see them. He had really missed them this past month, and he hoped they had missed him, too.

But they hadn't missed him. During the time they were away, those brothers spent a lot of time talking about Joseph. They talked about the new colorful coat. They talked about the dreams, and how Joseph thought he would one day rule over them. They talked about how Jacob loved Joseph more than them.

By the time the brothers had talked about all these things for a whole month, their bitterness toward Joseph had grown terrible. Now they saw him in the distance. Just the sight of him smiling and waving, wearing that coat, made their blood boil! And from somewhere, deep in the heart of first one brother, then another, came the dark desire to kill Joseph.

At first no one actually came right out and said it. "Here comes our brother, the dreamer," said Simeon. "He's probably crowned himself king since we've been gone."

"He had Father practically worshiping him before we even left!" Judah reached for a twig dangling just above his head. "The way he strutted around in that silly coat. . . ."

"I'd like to get my hands on that coat," jeered Asher. "I'd rip it to shreds! And I'd like to do it right in front of Joseph's eyes!"

"I'd like to rip Joseph to shreds!" Levi laughed when he spoke, but only for a second. He stopped and stared hard at the horizon where Joseph's still distant figure came closer. The group grew very quiet. Each brother was also gazing toward Joseph, lost in his own evil thoughts.

Simeon's voice was soft and raspy, "It could happen." Again there was a long silence. "There could be an . . . accident."

"They say that the animals that roam these hills attack without warning. I would hate for a wolf to get him," said Gad. "If that happened, there would be nothing left of him. Nothing. There wouldn't even be a way to prove that's what killed him."

"We could easily kill him and throw his body in one of these cisterns. As far as anyone else knew, a ferocious animal—"

Judah's planning was interrupted by Asher. "You mean we'd actually kill him ourselves?"

"Well, I don't know of a wolf on hand who would be willing to do the job for us," chuckled Levi.

"I say let's get rid of him. Then we'll see what comes of his dreams!" said Gad. "He won't do much ruling after he's dead!"

The other brothers eagerly agreed.

Only Reuben had been quiet during their planning. "Which one of you is going to tell Father?" They all grew quiet. "Which one is going to actually deal the fatal blow? Who wants to take the responsibility of killing one of our brothers?"

Suddenly the frenzied excitement was gone. But Reuben wasn't finished. "I say we don't take his life. Let's not shed any blood."

The others began to feel ashamed of their evil plans. They stared silently at the ground. It was quite a surprise, then, when Reuben made his next comment. They had expected him to rebuke them. Instead, he offered an alternative to the terrible deed they had wanted to commit.

"These cisterns are deep and remote. If Joseph were thrown into one, who knows when or if he would be found. We could still tell Father that an animal had devoured him. But we wouldn't actually be killing him—not directly anyway."

For a minute no one spoke. They were a little surprised that Reuben also wanted to be rid of Joseph.

They were also studying his new idea in their minds. Surely this would solve all their problems.

What the other brothers could not have known was Reuben's actual motive in suggesting this new plot. Reuben knew how his father felt about Joseph. He knew that it would be terribly wrong to actually kill Joseph. But Reuben also knew that killing Joseph was exactly what the others longed to do. As long as Joseph was around, his life would be in danger.

Reuben believed that the only way to save Joseph was to make his brothers think that they had gotten rid of him. Reuben then planned to come back and secretly rescue him from the cistern. Reuben felt sure that after he explained the dangerous situation, Joseph would flee from the brothers and never return. Now all Reuben had to do was find an excuse to leave them immediately. It was the only way he would be free to come back later to help Joseph.

"I will be the one to tell Father what has happened," said Reuben calmly. "But I must be able to say that I didn't actually see the animal. Otherwise Father will question how ten men were unable to fight off one wolf to defend Joseph's life. We must make it seem that the attack came while Joseph was alone."

Reuben waited a minute for his logic to sink in. "But I cannot lie to Father. That is why I can't be here among you when you throw him into the cistern."

The others readily agreed to his plan. Meanwhile, Joseph was getting closer and closer to them. Reuben quickly gathered his things and ran off toward the nearest clump of tall cedars. He made his way steadily toward the low hills. Unable to bear what was about to happen, he kept going long after he was safely out of Joseph's sight. He would stay away overnight. By the next day, the brothers would have started home with the sheep, and Reuben would set Joseph free.

Reuben stopped to rest on the rocky hillside. He felt awful. His stomach churned and his head ached. The evil talk about killing Joseph had made him sick. How had things gotten so bad? Reuben was also sick with worry. What if Joseph arrived at the brothers' camp and they decided to kill him anyway? They were still mad enough to do it!

Reuben's stomach felt sicker and sicker. He threw up several times that night. Sleep wouldn't come to relieve him. All he could think about was Joseph. What was happening back there at the camp? Would Reuben find Joseph frightened, but alive in the bottom of the cistern? Or would they kill him and bury him in a hidden grave? Joseph: alive—or dead?

10

AFTER walking for days and days to find his brothers, Joseph was exhausted. But when he had finally seen them in the valley below, his feet carried him quickly toward them. He was so happy to see them. He knew they would be glad that he brought news from Father and Leah. He couldn't wait to show them all the food she had sent! The closer he got, the faster his heart beat in happy anticipation.

At last Joseph was close enough to yell hello. The brothers scrambled to their feet and greeted him with smiles and friendly handshakes.

"Where's Reuben?" Joseph was sure he had seen his oldest brother from a distance. But now he was not among them.

"Oh, he took off after a wolf pup that has been bothering us for days. With any luck, he'll chase him off the face of the earth!" Levi laughed a little too heartily at his own comment. The others, too, laughed and glanced around nervously.

"So, how's Father?" Simeon seemed genuinely concerned. "And Benjamin?"

"They're both fine. And wait till you taste the meal Leah sent!" Joseph had removed the heavy pack from his back when he arrived. Now he went over and stooped to open it.

When he did so, three brothers grabbed him from behind. "Hey, cut it out! What's the idea?"

Joseph was knocked to the ground. At first, he thought they were just playing rough. But when they refused to let him up, he realized this was no game.

"Get his coat!" yelled Asher. "We'll need it later."

"Need it for what? What's going on? Get off of me!" Joseph was frantic. Why were they holding him down? Did they just want his coat? "Take the coat! You can have it! Just let me go!" But his cries were ignored.

The brothers stripped off his coat, jerked his hands behind his back, and tied them with rough strips of rope. Then they half-carried, half-pushed him over to where a dry cistern baked in the sun.

A long time ago a deep well had been dug around a natural spring. To keep the well from caving in and dirt falling into the water, the walls of the well had been lined with smooth rocks. Eventually the spring dried up. Now the old well was a cistern for holding water when rains fell during the rainy season. During summer months like these the well was dry.

Only the rock shaft remained. It was a long way to the bottom of the cistern. Had Joseph just been dropped into the cistern with his hands tied behind his back, he might have been killed when he hit the bottom. So Levi suggested that they tie a rope around his waist and lower him slowly.

Joseph's pleading had turned into sobs of panic. He was so confused and hurt. Why were his brothers doing this? What had he ever done to them? Would they just leave him in the cistern to rot away?

As they kept lowering him, the daylight grew dimmer. Joseph tried to struggle free, but his arms were bound by the rope around his waist. It dug into his stomach every time he breathed. If he didn't reach the bottom soon, he felt he would be cut in half!

Finally his feet touched the dank, soggy ground. He stumbled and fell to his knees in exhaustion. Far above him, at the mouth of the cistern, he heard the voice of his brother, Simeon.

"In case you want to climb out, you'll need a rope!" He heard the others laughing. They threw their end of the heavy rope down the shaft and it fell around Joseph like a dead snake.

"Come on," he heard them say, "lets see what's in that bag from Leah. I'm starved!"

Their laughter faded, and he knew they were leaving. An awful terror filled him. From somewhere deep inside, Joseph screamed. And screamed again.

He sobbed and coughed and sobbed some more. His screams had made him hoarse. He had no energy left at all. His life was ending here in this awful pit. It was cold. He was covered with wet, slimy mud.

Something smelled awful. As his eyes slowly adjusted to the darkness, he saw the decaying skeleton of an animal. It had probably fallen into the well, and like Joseph, was unable to climb back out. Maggots and flies covered the carcass and were slowly consuming it.

Through his tears Joseph stared blankly at the horrible sight. He tried not to think about what the maggots would eat next.

With no strength or hope left, Joseph slumped on the ground against the rock wall. Stagnant, watery mud had soaked through his clothes, and he was shivering with cold. It was hard to tell if he was awake or asleep, but it didn't make any difference. The pain he felt in his shoulders, hands, and stomach was nothing to compared to the misery he felt in his heart.

In the darkness he tried to imagine his father's face. Then Joseph remembered another time when he had felt this kind of despair. He almost laughed when he recalled those circumstances. A missing donkey, being lost on the hillside—oh, how he longed to be in that place of despair instead of this one.

But in remembering that time, Joseph also remembered asking for God's help. He had been crying just like now, and he had stopped and pleaded with God for help. Well, there was certainly no hope of getting God's help this time. Or was there?

Joseph couldn't even think of words that described how he felt. But he prayed anyway. No words, just tears, but they were directed at God.

Joseph let out a long sigh. The tears stopped and he forgot about his sore hands just long enough to fall asleep. Even if that sleep had been God's only answer to his prayer, it would have been alright with Joseph. For when he slept, there was no pain, no confusion, no terror. There was just sleep.

But that was not the only answer God had for his prayer. Somewhere in his half-sleeping mind Joseph heard the faint sounds of his brother's voices. At first he thought he must be dreaming. But the voices got louder. He heard Levi's familiar voice yelling to him, "Joseph? Joseph, are you still in there?"

Oh sure. Where else would he be? This must be further sport for the brothers. They just wanted to torment him some more. Joseph didn't answer them. *I won't give them the pleasure,* he thought. *I'll make them think I'm dead.*

But the voices continued. "Joseph, wake up. We've come to get you out! Can't you take a joke?"

A joke? If this was their idea of fun, Joseph failed to see its humor.

They kept talking. "We're throwing down another rope. Grab it and we'll pull you up."

That was funny. How was Joseph supposed to grab onto a rope with his hands behind his back? His brothers seemed pretty anxious to get him out. Joseph decided to see what they were up to. "If you want me, you'll have to come down and get me."

He heard them arguing among themselves. Some were saying to forget the whole thing and let him rot down there. But Simeon and Asher were determined to get him out. Joseph couldn't hear all that they said, but he heard the words, "slave" and "Egypt." Those were not words that made him feel comfortable. What was going on up there?

"We're coming down to get you!" said Simeon. Another rope swished down through the shaft and barely missed hitting Joseph on the head. In a few seconds he saw Levi scrambling down toward him with his knife clinched tightly in his teeth.

After landing with a thump, Levi moved quickly toward Joseph. For an instant, Joseph feared Levi would use the knife to kill him. But Levi simply cut away the excess rope tied around Joseph's waist. Then he tied the waist rope to the one which now dangled from above. Within a few seconds, Levi was straining to climb the rope back up the shaft.

"Hey, wait! You didn't even untie me!" Joseph stood up and called after the fast-disappearing Levi. There was no answer.

Without warning from above, the rope attached to Joseph's waist jerked hard. He fell forward, hitting his head against the rock shaft. They were going to pull him out with his hands still tied behind his back! His head hurt from the rocks, but Joseph knew that if he didn't watch out that they would sling him against the rocks with every pull.

It took every ounce of his strength to kick against the walls and keep from hitting the rocks. The rope cut into his middle, and he had to throw up.

Finally, when he thought he could stand no more, hands grabbed him and pulled him safely to the top of the well. His brothers hauled him over the edge and stood him up on his feet. The blood rushed to his head and Joseph fainted.

When he came to, he was lying under a tree. His eyes hurt from the bright sunlight. His hands were still tied behind his back. His head was bruised from hitting the rock, but at least he was free from his cistern prison. Joseph leaned back against the tree and closed his eyes. At least he was free.

But Joseph was far from free.

11

REUBEN was anxious to get back to rescue Joseph. But he must wait until the brothers had left with the sheep. It was now almost noon on the day after Joseph had been thrown in the well. Surely they would all be gone by now.

Reuben retraced his path. Cautiously he approached the grove of trees where they had last camped. Making sure that they had all left, he stopped and listened for sounds. Any sounds. There were none. The silence made Reuben nervous.

Running to the mouth of the well, Reuben peered anxiously down into the darkness. "Joseph! Joseph! Can you hear me? It's Reuben!"

There was nothing but silence. Reuben's heart pounded wildly. "Joseph! Please be in there! Please!" Again, nothing. "What have they done? Why did I leave! I could have fought to save him!"

Reuben, who was almost thirty years old, now dropped to his knees and sobbed like a child. The guilt he now felt would be with him the rest of his life.

Slowly he got to his feet. He must find his brothers. They must know what a terrible thing they had done. Reuben began to walk toward home. His heart was heavy and his steps were slow. How would they tell their father that his beloved son was dead?

Reuben didn't feel like eating, so he just kept on walking until it was too dark to see. The darkness of the sky could not match the darkness in his heart. He fell asleep and dreamed of Joseph.

The next morning Reuben caught up with his brothers and the sheep. He was shocked and angered to see the men who had committed murder two days before now laughing and joking beneath a shady tree.

"How could you do it? How could you just kill him?" Reuben voice quivered with grief.

"Kill him? You thought we killed him?" Asher had jumped to his feet in disbelief. "He's not dead! We couldn't really have killed him!"

"Well, where is he? If he isn't dead, why wasn't he in the cistern? Or why isn't he here?" Reuben was flooded with relief. Joseph was still alive!

"He's gone." It was a flat statement. Simeon was cool and matter-of-fact. "He won't bother us again."

Reuben's relief turned to fear again. "What have you done with him? Tell me!"

Slowly the truth was revealed. The brothers had lowered Joseph into the cistern as they had planned. Then, just as they were sitting down to eat the meal Leah sent, they saw a caravan in the distance.

At first they were scared that the men in the caravan would discover their cruelty to Joseph. But as the caravan neared, they saw that the men were Ishmaelites from Gilead. Heading for Egypt, the travelers had loaded their camels with spices and perfumes to sell.

It occurred to Judah that this might solve their problems. "Why don't we ask these men to buy Joseph? They'll take him to Egypt as a slave; we'll be rid of him without laying a hand on him. Let's sell him, instead of killing him. After all, he is our flesh and blood."

So when the merchants on their camels came by, the brothers had hauled Joseph up out of the cistern and sold him for 20 shekels of silver.

Reuben was stunned. He had thought Joseph was dead. Now he learned the horrible truth that Joseph had been sold—as a slave. What on earth would they tell Jacob now!

Taking Joseph's beautiful wool coat in his hands, Reuben tried desperately to come up with an idea. They had originally intended to lie to Jacob and tell him that a wolf had eaten Joseph. Fingering the soft wool in his hands, Reuben decided to use that lie now.

Killing a young goat, the brothers dipped the coat in some of its blood. Carefully they tore the coat, making it look like a terrible struggle had taken place. It was a quiet and solemn group of young men that began the slow, dreadful walk toward home.

Benjamin was the first to see them. "They're back, Father! All of them. They're coming over the hill!"

Jacob ran quickly from his tent into the bright sunshine. Shielding his eyes, he looked with joy and relief toward the horizon. Sheep stirred up the dry ground, making clouds of dust swirl around his sons. He could not see all of them clearly, so he began to count them.

Over and over he counted but could only come up with ten. Who was missing? His heart beat faster. *Please don't let it be Joseph! Let him be safe.* Would they never get close enough to know?

Reuben ran toward his anxious father. He said nothing. Holding Joseph's torn and bloody coat, he handed it to Jacob and looked away.

At first Jacob was silent. Then waves of grief swept over him. "It's Joseph's robe. Some terrible animal has torn him to pieces! Oh, Joseph, my Joseph. . . ."

Jacob fell to the ground sobbing and clutching the coat to his heart. None of the brothers were prepared for this moment. As the realization of what they had done began to sink in, each joined their father in tears. But they did not tell Jacob the truth.

Jacob wept for days. Benjamin tried to comfort his father, even though he was filled with sadness himself. How could this happen? If only he had been around, maybe he could have fought off the wolf. Now Joseph was gone. Benjamin's best friend was dead.

Life would never be the same. "I will mourn for Joseph until I die," groaned Jacob.

Sometimes late at night, Reuben lay in his tent unable to sleep. He wondered what had happened to Joseph. He tried not to think about his brother being a slave, but in the darkness of the tent his thoughts ran wild. Somewhere in Egypt, he knew, Joseph was suffering. All because of him. All because of them.

"Oh God!" he cried, "forgive us for what we did. Wherever Joseph is, please, God, please protect him."

And in the darkness of those lonely nights God heard that desperate prayer.

12

FOR a few minutes Joseph lay still under the tree. He was bruised and sick and sore but glad to be out of the cistern. Gradually he began to feel better and opened his eyes.

His brothers stood over him; that was a familiar sight. But there were other men, too. Men Joseph didn't know. These men weren't dressed like shepherds, and they spoke a language he didn't recognize. Nearby were about thirty camels loaded with brightly colored bundles and bags.

As Joseph studied this unusual sight, his brothers carried on a business conversation. One merchant took out a soft leather pouch and counted twenty silver coins into Reuben's outstretched hand. The merchant looked over at Joseph with a greedy smile that made Joseph's blood run cold.

In a few minutes Joseph's hands were tightly retied and he was hoisted on top of a seated camel. When the beast stood, Joseph had to hold on with his bound hands to avoid tumbling off. He was unsure what language these men spoke, but he knew exactly what had happened. His own brothers had sold him as a slave!

He called out to Simeon, "Don't let them take me, please!" But Simeon would not even look at him.

Joseph was too tired to keep fighting. The merchants prepared to leave with their cargo, including their newest purchase, a seventeen-year-old Hebrew slave. They hoped he would bring a nice profit in Egypt.

The journey began in the heat of the afternoon. Joseph's head was uncovered, and the sun poured down on him like hot water. He was so thirsty. He called to the man who walked in front of his camel.

"I need some water! Please! Just a drink of water." Lifting his tied hands up to his mouth, Joseph gestured for a drink.

The man stopped the camel and turned to look up at Joseph. He was a skinny old man, and his face was leathery from a lifetime of sun. Joseph waited to see if he had understood the request. The old man smiled and whistled to the others. He spoke to them in that same funny language.

To Joseph's great relief, one of the men took a wooden ladle and dipped it into a heavy pouch of water tied to a camel's back. The skinny old man lifted the ladle up for Joseph to drink. The water was warm from the afternoon sun, but it tasted wonderful to his parched tongue. Joseph smiled and thanked the man. After all, he could have refused to give Joseph a drink.

The old man even smiled back at Joseph. Then he took a long cloth from a pack on the camel and handed it to Joseph. Using two hands together, Joseph managed to wrap the cloth loosely around his head, shielding him from the searing heat. They walked on.

The camel rocked forward and back in a rhythmic motion. Before long, Joseph began to fall asleep. Once he dozed off and almost fell from the camel's back. With his hands tied, this would have been dangerous. From then on, he fought to stay awake. He found himself softly humming the songs his mother had sung to him when he was a little boy. They comforted him—and kept him awake.

Nightfall came and the caravan stopped. Joseph was allowed to eat with his hands untied, but the ropes were replaced before he went to sleep.

The next morning he was awakened and allowed to walk around for a few minutes before being lifted to the camel's back. The day wore on as the caravan moved slowly through the desert heat.

Joseph's thoughts went back to his home, where his brothers had probably arrived by now. What would they tell Jacob? Would he ever see his father again? Would his father miss him, too?

Each day began and ended the same way. Joseph rode on and on. His hands were raw underneath the ropes tying them together. The camel smelled terrible, and its stiff, scratchy hair rubbed Joseph's bare ankles. He lost count of the days, and had no idea how far they had traveled. He began to wonder if they were really headed somewhere, or if they would just wander around in the desert forever.

Finally one morning the caravan stopped beside a tiny oasis. The camels were allowed to drink for almost an hour. Even Joseph was removed from his perch and his hands were untied. All the merchants washed themselves in the water, and put on fresh clothes. They took off Joseph's dusty tunic and washed it thoroughly. His face was scrubbed and his hair combed.

"Why all the commotion?" he asked the skinny old man who had been his traveling companion. "Are we almost there?"

The old man smiled and pointed toward the horizon. Joseph didn't see a thing but sand. But the old man seemed to be telling him that their journey's end was just over the next hill.

"You must not want to sell a dirty slave!" Joseph laughed at the way the men were trying to comb his thick, wavy hair. "I'll do my best to make a fine showing." He pretended to model proudly, as if for a buyer.

The men from the caravan seemed to enjoy his relaxed performance. One of them, a short fat little man, came up to Joseph and tied a colorful sash around his waist. Joseph nodded in thanks.

Soon they were on their way again. In an hour the caravan stopped on a crest overlooking the valley below. The sights of the vast city stretched out before them. For a young boy raised among sheep and pastures, it was an exciting experience.

Egypt. Joseph had been brought to Egypt! All his life he had heard his father speak about this mysterious country. What would Jacob have thought if he had known that Joseph now stood on Egyptian soil?

Joseph was silent as he gazed at these new and wonderful sights. His heart raced. What lay ahead for him there? He was to be sold as a slave. Would he have to spend the rest of his life in chains?

Only God knew. In that final quiet moment, Joseph closed his eyes and spoke to his God. *You have been with me when I needed you before. You have even answered my prayers. Please, God, be with me now! Help me to know what your purpose is for me here in Egypt.*

The fat man whistled and the caravan lurched forward. The next time it stopped would be in the heart of that great city.

13

JOSEPH had never been inside a real city before. The caravan bumped and jostled its way through the narrow, crowded streets. On either side merchants had set up tables or carts full of things they wanted to sell.

Vegetables, wooden bowls, colorful cloths, and animals competed for the buyer's eye. Beggars wandered alongside the camels as they trudged forward. The smell of bread and spices and rotting fish filled the air. It was noisy. It was confusing. It was wonderful!

Near the center of the market area, the caravan came to a stop. The skinny old man convinced Joseph's camel to drop to its knees. Joseph quickly dismounted and stretched his stiff legs.

He was led to a group of men seated under a large canopy. They were well-dressed and clean. Sensing their prominence, Joseph immediately straightened and threw his shoulders back. He held his head high as he approached.

"How old is he?" One man, named Potiphar, had stood to ask the question in the Egyptian language.

The fat old man, who proved to know Joseph's language, translated the question for Joseph.

"I am seventeen, sir," Joseph said, and the fat old man relayed his answer to Potiphar.

Potiphar continued to look at Joseph. He studied his tall, erect body and muscular arms. He looked into Joseph's clear eyes. This young man was not only strong, he was intelligent as well.

Joseph, listening to the sharp interchange that now erupted between Potiphar and the fat old man, knew they must be bargaining.

The old man wiped sweat from his pudgy face. He jabbered on. His tone remained sharp but an undertone of resignation soon entered it. The deal was near, Joseph sensed.

He was right. Potiphar, grinning broadly, paid the fat little man, who went off grumbling to himself. Then Potiphar turned to Joseph.

"You carry yourself well," he said through the interpreter. "I am pleased. Just remember that as a slave you are to serve me upon my command. Do you understand?"

"Yes, sir." Joseph's voice mixed dignity, respect, and submission.

His new master was impressed. Potiphar suspected this young man would be of great value to him. But it would be necessary to prove that he could be trusted. A dishonest slave was worth nothing.

First the new slave would be taught the Egyptian language and enough of Egyptian ways to make his way freely through his master's household and lands. Then Potiphar would watch to see just how loyal Joseph might be.

Leaving the shade of the canopy, Joseph and his new master walked toward a waiting cart. Climbing into the cart, Potiphar instructed a servant to see that Joseph arrived safely at home. Two young boys quickly picked up the cart front and trotted off down the narrow street. Joseph was left standing with his hands still tied beside an old, gray-headed man. The man was apparently one of Potiphar's longtime servants.

Joseph looked directly into the old man's dark eyes. He waited for further instructions. The old man studied Joseph for a moment before instructing the interpreter what to tell Joseph.

"My master has done well with this latest purchase," he said in Egyptian.

Being called a purchase bothered Joseph a little, but he said nothing.

"Your duties will center around Potiphar's house. He is a very busy and important man. As captain of the guard, and one of Pharaoh's officials, he requires complete loyalty from those who serve him. He is often in the company of other prominent officials and frequently attends to Pharaoh's affairs himself."

As the old man spoke, Joseph noticed the excitement and pride in his voice. Here was a man who obviously admired and respected his master greatly.

"What will my duties be?" Joseph was anxious to prove that he could be trusted, and that he was a hard worker.

The old man listened to the translated words, then

thought for a moment. "To begin with, you will work in his house. There are several women who tend to the housekeeping, but occasionally there are tasks which require the strength of a man."

Joseph felt a familiar disappointment. He remembered his first trip with his brothers. Reuben had put him in charge of the donkey, and Joseph was humiliated. Now he felt the same humiliation. Working with the housekeepers! Surely there was a more worthy job for him than that!

Unfortunately, he was in no position to argue. Joseph simply replied, "I am willing to do whatever is asked of me." He meant it. Even if he was only doing the work of a woman, he would do it well.

It was a long walk through the city streets back to the home of Potiphar. Strong stone walls and heavy wooden gates surrounded the house. It was easy to see that Potiphar was an important man.

Joseph found it hard to believe that such extensive grounds were actually located in the heart of a bustling city. Once inside the gates, Joseph was impressed with the beauty and order of the grounds, as well as the main house. There were servant's quarters and guardhouses, and barns. All the buildings were made of heavy stone blocks, secure and stately.

Guards stood like statues outside each door. Secretly Joseph wished that he could be a guard. They looked so courageous. In his mind, he saw himself proud and erect on the battlefield.

But then he remembered what his real duties were to be. Seeing himself hauling dirty water like a maid was depressing. It was a good thing Joseph's brothers wouldn't be around to see him like this. He would have never heard the end of their laughter!

Over the next few weeks, Joseph immersed himself not only in the household tasks but learning the language and ways of the people who owned him. His depression gradually lifted. His quick mind enjoyed the challenge of absorbing new words and phrases and customs. He was soon able to understand his masters when they used simple words and before long he could answer for himself in this exciting new language.

One day the old servant who had first led him to Potiphar's house came for him and led him to the main house. "Wait here," the old servant commanded. "I will return for you in a moment. You will soon be meeting my master's wife." The man disappeared into the main house, leaving Joseph standing outside.

The master's wife. Joseph had heard of her but had not yet seen her. He wondered what she would be like. He pictured her as a plump, overbearing matron, capable of barking orders to the soldiers themselves. It was an amusing thought. Joseph laughed to himself. He never realized that this wife of his master, whoever she was, would bring still more trouble into his life.

The grand doors opened, and Joseph was ushered into the house. Waiting for him in the next room was Potiphar's wife.

14

THE mental picture of a plump, overbearing matron disappeared the instant Joseph saw the wife of his master, Potiphar. She was young and beautiful. She rose from a pile of silk cushions and glided gracefully toward him. Her dark hair was carelessly held back from her face with ivory combs. She wore white robes, which fluttered as she sailed across the room.

"You are the Hebrew servant my husband purchased?" Joseph took in a sharp breath at the sound of her smooth voice. She looked at him carefully, as though examining a bolt of cloth for flaws.

"Yes." It was the only response he could think of. Suddenly he felt like a piece of meat on display in the open market. Embarrassed, he glanced away.

"I am pleased that you have learned our language. You will be of great help to the household. Has Rahm taught you your duties?" Her deep brown eyes gazed at him, but her voice was strictly business.

"Yes. I have been helping the household servants with difficult chores. I am strong and willing to do whatever is needed."

"Good. You will continue your labors. Today the gardens are being reworked. There are some large stones that need to be removed."

Joseph nodded and turned to leave. But she spoke again, and he stopped in his tracks.

"My husband is a very important man. You will do well to remember that loyalty, honesty, and discretion are required of all who work for him. Is that clear?" There was no mistaking the tone in her voice. She was the master; he was the servant.

Joseph looked directly into her eyes and replied calmly, "Very clear." Then he went outside.

For the remainder of the afternoon he worked in the garden, hauling load after load of heavy stones that had once served as dividing borders. He was hot and tired, and finally sat down under a grape arbor to rest.

From where he sat, he could see the entrance to the guardhouse. One soldier stood guard at the door. As Joseph watched, another soldier came from the main house. The two men spoke softly and glanced around nervously. They did not see Joseph.

Then something strange happened. The soldier who had come from the main house took a scroll from inside his tunic and secretly handed it to the soldier at the guardhouse door. Now the guardhouse soldier hid the scroll inside his own tunic.

Joseph was curious. Why would two of Potiphar's guards be acting in such a secretive way? What was on that scroll? Where had it come from? Well, it wasn't any of his business.

That night, after dinner, the servants were called from their quarters to the main house. Joseph stood with them as they listened to a furious master.

Potiphar's voice trembled with rage. "Which one of you has been in my office today? Which one!"

He glared hard at his confused staff of servants, who stood meekly in the hallway. No one dared answer. Their silence only infuriated Potiphar more.

"Someone has been here! Someone has entered this office and removed an important document! I demand to know who it was!" Again there was silence.

"I should hate to have to punish all of you for the crime committed by only one person!"

When Potiphar said "one person" he looked directly at Joseph. The truth became painfully clear to Joseph. He was the real suspect. After all, he had only been with Potiphar's staff for a few weeks. For all they knew, Joseph might be a spy, a thief, or worse!

Taking a deep breath, Joseph gathered his courage to speak. "May I talk to you in private, sir?"

Hearing these words, the other servants gasped. He really must be guilty, they thought.

Potiphar's eyes were like cold steel when he looked at Joseph. "Yes. We will speak in private in my office."

Inside Potiphar's office, a small lamp stood on a low table. On the table were several scrolls, just like the one Joseph had seen earlier. Potiphar now stood facing Joseph, waiting.

But before Joseph could open his mouth to speak, the door opened and a guard entered the room. It was the very same guard Joseph had seen coming from the main house that afternoon! This guard had given the scroll to the man at the guardhouse door!

"Sir, I have questioned each of the soldiers in the guardhouse. No one knows anything about the missing item." The guard, standing straight and tall before his superior officer, was telling him a lie!

Joseph felt his heart beat wildly. What should he do? Would Potiphar take the word of this trusted guard, or would he believe the word of this young, almost unknown Hebrew slave?

"Thank you. That will be all," Potiphar dismissed the guard, then turned to face Joseph again. "What have you to say?"

Joseph waited for a brief moment before speaking. He was nervous but he didn't want his voice to be shaky. Finally, he took a long breath and began. "I know that I have not had a chance to earn your trust. But I am not only innocent, I also know who took the scroll." Then Joseph told Potiphar what he had seen as he sat unnoticed under the grape arbor.

At first Potiphar refused to believe this incredible story. But the more he listened, the more he realized it could be true. He decided to see for himself whether or not the two guards were guilty.

Potiphar dashed out of the house and entered the guardhouse unannounced. A thorough search of the door guard's belongings revealed that the scroll was there. It had been stolen by the very soldier sent to question the men at the guardhouse. Potiphar was enraged at being betrayed by two of his own guards. He sent them immediately away.

Inside the house, Joseph waited. Had he done the right thing? Soon Potiphar returned to the room.

"The two men in question have been dealt with. The scroll has been returned to me. Thank you. That was a courageous thing you did. It would have been easy enough to remain silent and still not be blamed."

Potiphar told Joseph to sit. He asked Joseph about his background, for here was a young man who had clearly been taught the value of loyalty and courage.

Joseph told Potiphar many things that night. He told him about his family, and his father's devotion to God. He told him about being dropped into the cistern, and about his prayer for rescue.

As Potiphar listened to this remarkable story, his admiration and fondness for Joseph grew. Surely Joseph's God was with this young man.

Joseph proved worthy of Potiphar's trust and high expectations. For the next six years, Joseph served in Potiphar's house. In the beginning, he did the simple chores he had been bought to do. But as the weeks and months went by, Potiphar began to rely on him more and more. Joseph solved problems so efficiently that Potiphar found it easy to turn over many of the household responsibilities to him.

Before long, Joseph was making decisions on his own, leaving Potiphar free to concentrate on his duties for Pharaoh. Potiphar put Joseph in charge of even more things, and was pleased to see that the household was running more smoothly than ever.

Working so closely with Potiphar, Joseph became more like a close friend than a servant. Yet he never forgot the reason for his success. Joseph knew that he was alive because of God's answer to his prayer in the cistern. There was some reason that God had brought him to Egypt. Perhaps it was only to be of help to this man named Potiphar. Joseph didn't know for sure. But he had learned to depend on God more and more.

Every day, no matter how busy or tired he was, Joseph made time to pray. When he was younger, he called on God only when he needed help. Now that he was older, he talked to God about everything—his hopes and fears, his questions, his dreams.

Joseph's life in Egypt was pleasant and rewarding. Potiphar was a very rich man, and Joseph, who no longer lived in the servant's quarters, had been given a room in the beautiful main house. He spent his days walking on cool marble floors or among lush green gardens. He ate well at Potiphar's table, and wore the expensive clothes Potiphar provided for him.

Yet sometimes late at night, Joseph's thoughts drifted far from this fine Egyptian palace. He closed his eyes and tried to remember the sounds of a crackling fire at breakfast. He remembered the smell of his heavy goats' hair tent and the rough scratchy blankets he used to sleep under. He remembered Leah's heavy barley-fig bread, and how she sang when she spun the wool from the sheep.

But most of all, Joseph remembered his father. Even in the darkness so many years later, he could still see Jacob's tangled white beard, his rough, leathery hands, his steady eyes.

What had happened to his family by now? Was Benjamin now a young man? Did his older brothers have children of their own? Was Jacob even alive? There were no answers for him in the dark night of Egypt. He wondered if he would ever know the answers.

15

ONE day, when Joseph was out in the garden, a guard brought him a message. "Your master wishes to speak with you in his office," the young guard said.

Joseph had been working on plans for a new water system, but when he learned Potiphar wanted to see him, he immediately went into the main house. Inside it was cool. Joseph washed his hands and face and combed his hair before entering Potiphar's office.

"Come in, Joseph, come in!" Potiphar stood up and stretched. He had been sitting for a long time. "I have just been reviewing my orders from Pharaoh. He will be sending some of my men to Memphis to train new soldiers there. I must go down with them."

Joseph waited patiently for Potiphar to come to the reason for wanting to see him. Secretly Joseph was hoping he would be needed in the training. He longed to join the guard, although he knew that would be impossible for him as a Hebrew.

"I will be gone almost a month," Potiphar continued. "I am putting you in charge. I'm sure you will do well—you have proven yourself many times."

A whole month! Joseph was flattered to be placed totally in charge. Potiphar had never been away for more than a few days. Harvest season was approaching, and there was still much work to do on the new water system. It would be a busy time for Joseph.

"You do not need to worry, sir. I will see that everything runs smoothly while you are away. I will also ask God to bless you with safe travel and success on your trip." Joseph remembered his father's prayers for every journey.

"Thank you, Joseph. Now, I have much to do. I will leave early in the morning." Potiphar turned to his work.

The soldiers gathered at daylight next morning. Those who would not be going were given various orders and put under command of the captain's assistant.

Potiphar kissed his lovely wife, Annet, good-bye. Joseph stood near the door to the main house. He noticed that Annet did not seem too saddened at her coming separation from her husband. Perhaps she was just putting up a brave front for him. Still, it made Joseph wonder.

The soldiers left. It was an impressive sight. The polished handles of their swords caught the morning sun and flashed like lightening. The rhythmic sounds made by marching feet made Joseph sigh with envy. Maybe someday. . . .

Right now there were chores to be done. He was determined to run Potiphar's house efficiently. Pausing just long enough to instruct the servants on their morning duties, Joseph was soon deeply involved in the water system plans. For several hours he worked alongside the other men digging a maze of shallow trenches that would later be lined with smooth rocks.

The afternoon sun grew hot, so they stopped to rest. Joseph went into the house to eat a bite of lunch. Since it was past lunchtime, the cook had left a plate of roasted meat and some bread under a cloth on the table. Helping himself, Joseph was just sitting down to eat when Potiphar's wife, Annet, came into the room. He stood up at once, for a servant should never remain seated when in the presence of a master.

"No, Joseph, please sit down and eat your lunch," Annet motioned for him to sit. She went to the table and poured herself some juice from a small pottery pitcher. Then, to Joseph's surprise, she sat near him.

"Tell me, Joseph, how is your work going on the new water system?" Her eyes sparkled with interest.

"It is going well," he began. "It will take a long time to dig all of the trenches. After that, the work should go quickly. Most of the stones have already been cut." He wasn't sure just how much she wanted to know.

"I'm sure that you'll get it finished before my husband returns," Annet smiled at Joseph.

She was making him nervous. While she was often in the room when Potiphar discussed things with Joseph, she had seldom spoken to him alone.

He stood. "Excuse me, I have much work to do."

Once outside, Joseph quickly returned to the difficult task of digging. He soon put the conversation with Annet out of his mind.

The next morning, the men resumed their work while it was still cool. They worked through the morning without a break. Joseph was pleased with the progress they were making.

"Surely you must be thirsty by now!"

It was Annet. She had walked quietly up behind him and stood in the middle of the workmen. She was holding a silver tray. On it were fresh pastries and two silver cups filled with juice.

Without waiting for further encouragement, Annet spoke to the other workmen, "The servants have prepared some bread and drinks for you in the courtyard." Setting her tray down on the grass near Joseph, she dismissed the men with a wave of her hand.

Not knowing what else to do, Joseph joined Annet. She graciously served the pastries as she asked questions about the water system.

"Joseph, where did you learn to be so creative?"

He had no answer.

She went on, "I know that you must think I'm terribly silly, but I find your work fascinating! I hope you don't mind my coming out to watch."

He did mind. When Annet was around, the workmen were so distracted they hardly got anything done. But Joseph couldn't think of a way to discourage her. Why should she be so interested in a water system anyway? He was beginning to be annoyed with her.

But day after day she came out to watch. She asked a thousand questions. Joseph patiently answered each.

Then she began to follow him when he tried to get work done around the grounds. Everywhere he went, there she was, usually with a tray of food or something cool to drink. His nerves were fraying.

One day when he was resting under the grape arbor, he looked up to see her standing over him. "You startled me! I didn't know you were there!"

When will she stop these little games! Joseph thought, furiously.

She giggled. "What were you thinking about, Joseph?" Annet plopped herself down right beside him.

"Nothing." His voice was curt.

"I don't believe you," she said. "I'll bet you were secretly thinking about me!"

"Why would I be thinking about *you*?" He didn't mean to sound quite so hateful, but he did.

"I just thought that maybe, sometimes, you might wonder about me, that's all." She sounded a little hurt but plowed ahead anyway. "After all, my husband will be away for a long time. I'm bound to get . . . lonely. Tell me, Joseph, don't you ever get lonely?"

He took a deep breath and said, "When I am lonely, I always talk to God. It helps me not to feel so alone."

Clearly this was not the answer that Annet was looking for. She tilted her head back and laughed. "No, Joseph, I don't mean that kind of lonely! I mean for someone to hold."

Joseph stood quickly to avoid Annet's trap. "I'm sorry. I've got some work to do. Please excuse me."

He turned and ran down the path toward the gardens. He didn't stop running until he had reached the spot where the other workmen had stopped to eat.

"What's the matter, Joseph?" one of them said. "You look like you've had a good scare!" The others laughed and asked him if he had seen a skeleton. But Joseph was not in a laughing mood. He tersely ordered them back to work. Nothing more was said about the matter.

That night, Joseph avoided Annet altogether. Usually he had dinner in the kitchen, but tonight he took his supper and went quietly to his room.

He couldn't sleep. The full moon shone into his room as if it were midday. Finally, tired of tossing on his bed, Joseph got up and went to the wide ledge of the window. He sat there a long time, staring at that bright moon, wondering just what had happened to-day.

Why had Annet been following him so closely late-ly? Was she really interested in his work, or was she just lonely since Potiphar had been gone? Maybe she just needed someone to talk to.

But Joseph knew that there was more to it than that. He had seen the way she looked at him. And today, under the grape arbor, she had actually come right out and said, "lonely for someone to hold." There was no mistaking what she wanted.

The most frustrating part for Joseph was that he found himself thinking about holding her. She was so beautiful, so young, so . . . willing! Joseph had never held a woman before, but it was something that he wanted very much to do.

For a moment, he imagined holding Annet, kissing Annet. Potiphar would never have to know. He would be gone for several more days. Maybe. . . .

"God help me!" cried Joseph softly. "She is Potiphar's wife. I cannot hold her. I must not! God, please give me the strength to say no to her. I am so tempted. But it would be so wrong."

16

THE next few days passed quickly. Annet was not following Joseph around like she had earlier. As a result, Joseph and the rest of the workers were getting a lot done. He began to relax. Maybe he had misunderstood. Maybe she had only wanted a friend to talk to. Joseph decided to forget about it.

But although Joseph was trying to put the matter completely out of his mind, Annet could think of nothing else. She had fallen in love with Joseph from the moment he had walked into her house six years ago. A tall, young muscular boy then, he had swept her off her feet and didn't even know it.

Now he was a grown man. If anything, he had become even more handsome. He was intelligent and had a gentle manner about him that her own Potiphar lacked. Potiphar could never give her the affection and warmth she felt certain Joseph could give.

Annet was used to having her own way. She had always gotten exactly what she wanted. Now she wanted

Joseph. She had to have him. She just had to!

One night, after supper, Annet caught sight of Joseph walking alone down the path toward the garden. She quickly went to her room and brushed her hair. She put on a lovely silk robe and rubbed perfumed lotion on her face and hands. Then she quietly darted out the door and down the path.

Joseph was sitting on a stone bench, deep in thought. For a moment, Annet stood in the dark shadows behind a tree. She studied him. The soft moonlight fell on his broad shoulders. He ran his hand through his dark hair. The very sight of him made her breath harder.

Silently, she crept up behind him, and gently put her arms around his neck. Startled, he jumped to his feet.

"Annet! What are you doing out here?"

"I just wanted to be with you." She was facing him now, and he had never seemed so tall or so strong as he did at this moment. Her heart beat wildly! She put her arms around him again, but this time she was so close she could feel him breathing.

"Joseph, please kiss me." She turned her face up, waiting.

But Joseph took a step back. Gently but firmly he reached behind his neck and removed her hands. Holding them tightly down at her side, he looked at her for a moment before he spoke.

"No, Annet. No, I won't. Listen to me. Potiphar has put me in charge of everything he owns. He has placed his trust in me. He has withheld nothing from me except you, because you are his wife. To hold you and kiss you would be wrong, Annet. I can't do that to Potiphar. And how could I sin against my God like that?" Joseph's voice was strong, but not loud. He looked straight into Annet's eyes—and saw tears mixed with growing rage.

He was embarrassed for her. He felt awkward standing there, so he turned and walked away from the garden. He went back to his own room and fell onto his bed. The confidence and control he had displayed for her benefit were now gone. He put his hands over his face and sighed. God really had provided the strength.

Two days later the household busily prepared for Potiphar's return. No one knew exactly what time of day he would be back, so the welcome feast was planned for the evening meal. All day servants bustled in and out with large trays of meats and exotic fruits and wines. The silver was polished and the candles replaced. Everything sparkled.

Everything, that is, except Annet. There were dark circles under her eyes. Her hair, which was usually gleaming and soft, was pulled back into a severe, oily bun. Her face was puffy, and she was a grouch. Nothing suited her. She barked orders at the servants and criticized their every move. Finally she sent them all to their quarters to await Potiphar's return.

Joseph had spent most of the day in the gardens. The water system had been completed and was finally working smoothly. Joseph looked forward to the proud moment when he could show off this accomplishment to Potiphar.

He was standing in the shade admiring the sight of the gently flowing water when a servant approached him. "The master's wife wishes to see you inside."

Joseph, having heard what kind of mood Annet was in, boyishly rolled his eyes. The servant giggled in delight.

All the way up to the main house, Joseph wondered what Annet could want. She had been completely silent the last two days. He was relieved that Potiphar would be home soon. Then this unpleasant business would end.

Once inside, Joseph couldn't find any servants. It seemed strange that they should all vanish when there was so much work to do in preparation for tonight. He didn't know where Annet was, so he decided to wait for her in the formal room.

This was a beautiful room where guests were received. Its marble floors reflected the light from soft candles in their sparkling silver holders. Ornate tapestries hung from the walls, and silk cushions were tossed in giant heaps on the rugs. It was from one of these piles of cushions that Annet had risen to greet Joseph the first time he had entered Potiphar's house.

Seeing that picture in his mind as he entered the room, Joseph was completely startled to see Annet reclining on those same cushions this very minute. Before he could say anything, she quickly stood and ran to him. All the youthful beauty that had taken Joseph by surprise on that first day was now gone. Before him was a desperate woman.

As she approached him, she said, "Joseph, my husband will return today. But it is not Potiphar I long for. It is you. Take me, Joseph!" She ordered hoarsely. She grabbed his outer robe.

Joseph backed up, but she held on. Finally he pushed her away from him and ran toward the door. The robe came loose and remained clenched in her fist. Joseph caught a glimpse of Annet's arm held in midair with the robe hanging limply, like something she had killed. Her other hand was across her forehead. She was trembling as furious, frustrated tears rolled down her face.

Then Joseph raced from the room and fled to his quarters for another robe. Annet's actions had shaken him deeply. He needed time to think.

Joseph quietly made his way down the grand marble stairs and out into the cool gardens.

He sat down beside a well and closed his eyes, hoping that the terrible ordeal he'd just been through would go away.

He was lost in thought when he heard loud noises. There was a great commotion going on near the front wall. A young servant boy had spotted Potiphar's carriage near the outside gates. Potiphar was home!

Joseph quickly washed his face with well water and ran his hands through his hair. It was time to face his master. What would Potiphar say if he ever found out the truth about his wife? Would Potiphar ever know the truth?

17

JOSEPH heard screams. They were a woman's screams. Turning from the shady well and looking at the main house, he was alarmed to see people running toward the door. Still more screams, and Joseph recognized the voice of Annet. She was the woman screaming. Something terrible must have happened!

Joseph wasted no time getting up to the main house. What could have happened to make Annet scream so dreadfully? He had just reached the door when someone grabbed him from behind. Jerking his head around, he was surprised to see one of Potiphar's guards.

"I've got him. I've got him right here!" The guard called out to some other soldiers nearby. Two of them rushed up and helped hold Joseph tighter. The others ran inside.

"What's the matter with you? It's Joseph! Don't you recognized who I am?" Joseph squirmed to get loose, but the guards only strengthened their grip. "What's going on here?" He was starting to get angry. Why were they holding him?

In a moment Potiphar himself stepped out onto the veranda where the guards were holding Joseph. One look at Potiphar's face and Joseph forgot his struggle to get free. Never had Joseph seen such a look on this man's face. Potiphar was seething with rage, and his eyes seemed to shoot bolts of fire at Joseph. But there was something else in that face. Somehow, beneath all the anger, there was a sad, almost questioning look.

"Bring him inside at once!" Potiphar's voice shook with emotion. Although he had no clue why he was being treated like a criminal, Joseph was suddenly very frightened. He went along without fighting.

Once inside, Joseph's attention immediately went to the center of the formal room. Several servants knelt beside a bed of silk cushions. There was a woman lying on the cushions; for a moment Joseph didn't know who it was. When a servant stood, Joseph saw the woman's face. Annet! She looked terrible. Her clothes were torn. Scratches showed on her bare shoulders. Her hair was wild and matted. Her face had no color, except for the dark circles under eyes.

"What has happened? What's wrong with Annet?" Joseph looked at Potiphar. "She's been hurt. Who has done such a thing?"

Potiphar reached down for something tossed in a heap on the floor. He held up Joseph's robe in a shaking fist. Staring at it as if it was something venomous, he shook it in Joseph's face.

"Who has done such a thing?" He seemed unable to

speak through his fury. "Who has done such a thing!" yelled Potiphar. "Tell me, Joseph, who owns this robe, and I will tell you who has done such a thing!"

"It's mine, but I—" There was no chance to finish.

"Get him out of here. Get him out of this house!" Annet had risen up from her pillow and pointed a quivering finger at Joseph. She fell back in sobs.

The guards still holding Joseph started to push him toward the door. He tried to turn back to face Potiphar, but was overpowered. "Potiphar, please! Tell me what has happened!" Joseph felt again the terror he once knew as his brothers shoved him toward the dry cistern.

"Stop," Potiphar halted the guards. They relaxed their hold on Joseph, who now stood face to face with his master.

Potiphar's voice was soft as he tried to control his anger. "I will tell you exactly what has happened. I left a month ago and placed you in charge of everything I owned. I trusted you with my entire household. This—" Potiphar stopped and held up the robe once more. "This is how you repay my trust."

Joseph waited, still in shock, yet beginning to suspect what a dreadful situation he now faced.

"You were not content to be in charge of my whole household," Potiphar continued. "You had to have the one thing that was forbidden. You had to have my wife!"

Joseph straightened. He stared at Annet. "I never touched your wife," Joseph gravely said.

"Liar!" Potiphar's voice boomed. "You tried to grab and kiss her. She fought back and you ripped at her clothing. Her screams scared you away. This robe proves it to be true!"

Joseph stared at Annet. He wanted her to tell Potiphar, and everyone else, that this was all untrue. But she lay on the cushions and would not look at him.

Now the situation became clear to Joseph. Her frustration had turned her against him. It was all an act! She was so humiliated that Joseph would not hold her and kiss her that she made up this horrible, ridiculous story. What was worse, Potiphar believed her.

"Potiphar, listen to me. I never—"

"Silence! Take him to Pharaoh's prison."

Joseph had awakened that morning in his own room in Potiphar's lovely house. He had been happy. He had been proud of the good job he had done in caring for his master's household. He had thanked God for continuing to bless him in such a special way.

But tonight Joseph lay on a hard, cold stone floor. His hands and feet were bound by iron cuffs and chained to the floor. He hadn't eaten all day. There was no window, and the air was stale and damp. All around him, other prisoners slept in chains, their soft moans making an eerie sound in the darkness.

Joseph couldn't sleep. He flinched from the hatred of this woman so determined to get revenge that she had caused him to be thrown into prison. Potiphar had believed her! Potiphar was Joseph's friend, yet he hadn't given Joseph a chance to defend himself. Would Potiphar ever know what really happened? That his own wife had wanted to kiss another man, a Hebrew slave? That she had lied to her own husband? What, Joseph wondered, would happen to him now?

Would he stay in this dingy prison forever?

Once again, there were no answers. But now Joseph was an adult. He no longer had to wonder how his father would handle a situation. Ever since he was a young boy, Joseph had come to God.

So now, even in that dark night, Joseph knew he must pray. Closing his eyes, he was silent for a moment. Then he spoke softly, "Lord God, you have allowed me to be placed here for a purpose. I am confused, and I am frightened. I have been treated unfairly. But somehow, I know that I will be alright. I know that you will show me what I am to do. Please help me, God, to be patient and to wait for the answers that only you can give. Amen."

Joseph went to sleep that night in prison. He knew that God had a plan for him. But in the meantime, he would have to stay where he was. He would have to stay in that prison for a very long time.

18

WHAT'S wrong with that old man?" asked Joseph.

"He won't eat." The prisoner seated next to Joseph didn't offer much of an explanation.

"Why not? He'll soon starve to death!" Joseph had watched the old man near him with growing concern. Joseph had only been in the prison three days, but every time a meal was served, this old man refused to touch any food. He only stared at his meals with vacant eyes. He didn't seem to notice or care that the other prisoners sitting around him stole the food off of his plate. But Joseph noticed, and it bothered him terribly.

"Why won't he eat anything?"

"He feels that he was put here unfairly." A young man about Joseph's age, named Talgar, shifted the heavy chains that held him to the floor. "Most of us feel that way."

Did they? Joseph certainly did! He had been put in prison solely because of the lying accusations of

Potiphar's wife. Joseph wondered how many of the other men in chains had similar stories. He suspected some were innocent like he was, but had no way of proving it. But what about this old man?

"The old fellow has lost his will to stay alive," Talgar continued. "He served as one of Pharaoh's personal attendants for many years. Some gold coins were missing from a bag in Pharaoh's chambers, and this faithful old servant was presumed a thief. Imagine being accused of such a crime when you have given so many years of your life to someone!"

"They never found out who really stole the coins?" Joseph was deeply interested in this story.

"No. The old man will probably die in here, and the real thief has probably left Egypt by now."

The more Joseph learned about this old man, the more concerned he became. At first, the old man refused to talk. His dark eyes stared blankly at the floor, not meeting the eyes of the other prisoners. But Joseph kept trying. He noticed that the old man's feet were turning purple from being pinched by the iron ankle cuffs. He asked the guard to adjust them, then Joseph spent several hours gently rubbing the rough, cold feet, trying to get warm blood circulating again.

As his feet began to warm up, so did the old man's heart. He looked at Joseph and even smiled. Gradually, with patience, Joseph even convinced him to eat some food. He would be alright now. Someone cared about him in this nasty place.

The old man wasn't the only person to benefit from Joseph's compassion. There were others who also had lost all hope. But Joseph encouraged them to talk about their lives. They didn't need to relive the horrible circumstances that had placed them in prison. They just began to think about the good times in their lives, and about the families that loved them still. It was as if Joseph offered a small spark of a flame that grew in each man near him, warming up some life where there had only been cold darkness before.

The chief jailer noticed the change in his prisoners. Although it was his job to keep them chained, he never enjoyed watching them suffer. His heart ached for the old man and for the others who lingered day after day in that hopeless place. But now that Joseph was there, everything was different.

"Joseph, you have a special way with these men."

"They only need someone who will listen." As usual, Joseph was uncomfortable with too much praise.

"No, Joseph," the chief jailer insisted. "It is far more than being a good listener. You seem to have a rare gift. I can't quite describe what it is."

"I think I can," Joseph was pleased to have won the chief jailer's approval. "It is a part of God's plan for me."

"Your God planned for you to be in *prison*?" The jailer looked at Joseph in surprise.

"Well, I don't know that my God actually put me in here, but I do know that God has promised to be with me wherever I am."

Joseph told the jailer about those times in his life when everything seemed to be going wrong. Each time, God had answered his prayers, and had seen him through the difficult times.

"Even here in prison," Joseph went on, "I know that

God has work for me to do. Perhaps it is just to encourage the other prisoners."

The jailer thought about Joseph's commitment to his God for several days after that conversation. He began to admire this young man more and more. The prison was being handled so smoothly, just because Joseph was there. The jailer gradually began letting Joseph handle some of the responsibilities. The other prisoners respected Joseph and were always willing to follow his example.

Whenever a problem came up, the jailer asked Joseph how to handle it. Joseph was wise and fair. He also inspired the other prisoners with his devotion to his God. Each night in jail, as he had each night of his entire life, Joseph spent a quiet time alone in prayer. His prayers were not heard by the others, but the prisoners somehow knew that Joseph's God was important enough for Joseph to set aside time to pray.

Days wore on in prison. Deep inside the heavy stone-walled building, no one kept up with passing time. Seldom did anything happen that was different or unusual. But one day, there was a commotion outside that startled even the prisoners.

19

"GET your hands off me!"

"Quiet, or I'll have you beaten before I toss you in jail!"

"You can't do this to us! We're personal attendants to Pharaoh himself!"

"You mean 'personal prisoners' of Pharaoh himself!" This remark was followed by gruff laughter from several prison guards.

The noise grew closer, until the door of the prison room was roughly kicked open and two men were shoved inside.

"Here. Now you can be personal attendants to this bunch of criminals," the guards slammed the door, leaving the two bewildered men standing in the middle of the room.

The chief jailer routinely placed the iron cuffs on their ankles and wrists and guided them over to a vacant spot near Joseph. As he was securing their chains to the floor with heavy iron pegs, Joseph got his first good look at the two men. He knew them!

Manaded, the chief baker, and Berraf, the Pharaoh's wine taster. What on earth could have happened to cause them to be thrown in jail? Joseph waited until they had calmed down before he turned to face them.

"Joseph!" Berraf was shocked to see a familiar face in this awful place. "Joseph, what is happening? Why are we here . . . in prison?"

His face was white with fear, and beads of sweat poured off his bald head. He was breathing so heavily Joseph was afraid he might faint at any minute.

"It's alright, Berraf. Just try to relax for a minute. You can tell me about it when you feel better."

Joseph was curious, but he knew Berraf's health had never been strong. Berraf leaned his head against the stone wall and closed his eyes.

Joseph knew what he must be thinking, for he had had the same thoughts himself when he first arrived here. *I can't be in prison, I just can't. Surely when I open my eyes again, I will see that it was all a nightmare!* But Joseph knew that when Berraf opened his eyes, he would see that he was not dreaming, he was indeed in prison.

Manaded was more in control of his emotions. He calmly explained that Pharaoh had become angry with both himself and Berraf. Apparently, someone had helped themselves to Pharaoh's wine supply one night. The next morning, several jars of wine had been taken, while others lay broken on the floor.

One servant was certain that he had seen Berraf near there that night. Another claimed that the chief baker, Manaded, had been too drunk to prepare the pastries for breakfast that morning. Since neither man could actually prove where he had been, Pharaoh had them both thrown in jail.

Berraf was feeling better now, and spoke to Joseph. "How long have you been in prison?" Joseph had to admit that he really didn't know.

Berraf admitted this made him uneasy. "Will I be in prison so long that I'll lose track of time too? I hope not!"

For the first time in several months, Joseph found himself wondering about Potiphar and Annet. Perhaps it was because these two new prisoners had just arrived from the outside, where the events of Pharaoh's kingdom were known to all the servants. Finally he could resist the temptation no longer.

"Tell me, Manaded, do you ever see my master, Potiphar?"

"Yes, I see him, or rather I *saw* him quite often when he came to meet with Pharaoh. He is fine, but there is something about him that has changed."

"I don't understand," said Joseph.

"It is hard to explain. Potiphar always used to seem so alive and hearty. Now he looks tired and almost sad all the time."

Joseph hesitated, then asked, "What about his wife, Annet?"

"No one ever sees her anymore. Apparently she has retired to her bedroom and seldom comes out. Even her servants say she is like an old woman who doesn't want to face life. No one knows why."

But Joseph knew why. Annet's life had been consumed by her love for Joseph. When he rejected her, she felt that her life had been destroyed. Then she had let her rage burn up any remaining beauty in her life. It made Joseph sad to think about her now. It seemed a tragic waste.

Manaded and Berraf gradually resigned themselves to prison life. They no longer grumbled about the unfairness that put them there. Instead, they grew to know and like the other prisoners, as Joseph had.

One morning, just after they had eaten breakfast, Joseph noticed that both Manaded and Berraf were unusually quiet. "Why the long faces? You two haven't said a word all morning."

Manaded spoke first. "I had a dream last night. My dreams don't usually bother me, but this dream was different. I can't explain it, but there was something special about it. There was some meaning behind it, but I don't know what."

"I had a dream, too!" exclaimed Berraf. "It has been troubling me ever since I woke. I feel like I'm supposed to know what the dream meant, and I haven't a clue. It's driving me crazy!"

"Somehow our dreams must have something to do with our futures," said Manaded. "If only there were someone who could interpret them!"

It distressed Joseph that his two friends were upset by their dreams. He remembered the day, long ago, when he had had his first special dream. He had known then that his dream was not ordinary. He wondered now if Manaded and Berraf's dreams were sent from God like his had been.

"Tell me your dreams. Interpreting dreams is something God can do. Maybe through God I will know what your dreams mean."

Berraf was anxious to hear how Joseph would explain his unusual dream. He spoke quickly, "Let me tell mine first. In my dream I saw a vine with three branches."

Chains rattled as Berraf struggled to hold up three fingers. "The branches were just beginning to bud and blossom, and soon I saw that they each had beautiful clusters of plump, ripe grapes! Now let me think what came next. . . ."

He squinted his eyes, deep in thought, then went on. "I was holding Pharaoh's wine cup in my hand, so I naturally took the grapes and squeezed the juice into the cup." This he demonstrated for Joseph.

"Then I gave it to Pharaoh to drink. . . ." Berraf's voice trailed off. He was lost in his thoughts.

While Berraf described his dream, Joseph was half listening, half praying for God's help. He had never really interpreted someone else's dream before, but suddenly the meaning to Berraf's dream seemed clear.

"I know exactly what your dream means, Berraf!" Joseph cried. "The three branches mean three days. In three days Pharaoh is going to take you out of this prison and give you back your job as his wine taster."

"Do you really think so, Joseph? Oh, that is wonderful. Just wonderful!" Berraf's voice reflected the huge grin on his face. His eyes sparkled with hope.

"Berraf," said Joseph quietly, "when you get out, please do something for me."

"Oh anything, Joseph. After all, it was you who interpreted this marvelous dream for me!"

"No, actually it was God," Joseph reminded Berraf. "Anyway, when you get out, I want you to speak to

Pharaoh when you are back in his favor. Mention my name to him, and ask him to release me, too. After all, I was kidnapped from my homeland, and sold as a slave. And now this!" Joseph held up both hands to show his heavy chains. "Here I am in prison, and I did absolutely nothing to deserve it."

"Don't worry, Joseph. I won't forget you," Berraf spoke with such gentle confidence that Joseph felt hopeful already.

When Manaded saw that Berraf's dream had meant such good fortune, he was anxious to tell his dream, too. He shifted uncomfortably under the weight of his chains. He was a very plump little man. Apparently he had frequently sampled the delicious baked goods he supplied to Pharaoh's table.

Manaded struggled to put into words the dream that he now hoped would be his ticket out of this prison. "My dream happened like this. There were three baskets of pastries on my head." He was interrupted by chuckles from Berraf.

Giving Berraf a cold look, Manaded continued. "Anyway, in the top basket were all kinds of delicious baked goods for Pharaoh," he paused and licked his lips. Just the thought of fresh hot pastries made his mouth water. "But then a bunch of birds came and ate them all."

Joseph frowned and didn't say anything for a minute. The meaning was clear to him at once, just as with Berraf's dream. But this time that meaning was not going to be a pleasant one.

"The three baskets mean three days," Joseph said slowly. He wasn't sure how to put the next part. "Three days from now Pharaoh will also remove you from prison."

Joseph heard Manaded gasp excitedly and flinched from the terror he knew Manaded was about to feel. "Manaded, Pharaoh will have you beheaded. He will hang your body on a pole. The birds will come and pick off all your flesh."

Manaded was silent. His eyes flew wide open, but he could not speak.

"Tell him it isn't so, Joseph!" Berraf was frantic. "It can't be!"

"I'm sorry, Manaded. This is the meaning God has given to your dream." Joseph's heart was heavy. He had no idea that interpreting dreams would be so painful. He saw the hope in Manaded's eyes die away.

The rest of that day, no one was in the mood to talk. Manaded couldn't decide whether to be angry with Joseph or to believe the dream's meaning. Either way, he was filled with despair.

Three days later, there was a great commotion at the guard's door. Two of Pharaoh's attendants had arrived with big news. The prisoners listened quietly to the conversation.

"Today is Pharaoh's birthday. He is hosting a huge party for all of his officials and household staff." The attendant went on to explain, "We have been sent to have the chief baker and chief wine taster released."

When Berraf and Manaded heard this, they could hardly contain their excitement. "We're free! Did you hear them, Joseph? We're to be released!" Manaded's round little body trembled with joy.

As the two men were escorted out of the prison cell,

Joseph's heart was filled with sorrow. He knew what was about to happen.

The next day, the jailer spoke quietly to Joseph. "It all took place just as you said. Pharaoh restored Berraf to his former position as wine taster, but as for Manaded—"

Joseph waited for the words he did not want to hear.

"Pharaoh determined that it was Manaded who had really stolen the wine. When he denied it, Pharaoh ordered that he be killed. His body is hanging on a pole for the birds to eat. It is horrible. Just horrible," the jailer walked away shaking his head sadly.

Joseph was so sad about the death of Manaded. He tried not to let his mind dwell on the image the jailer had described. Joseph forced himself to think about Berraf.

Now that Berraf was free, he would surely remember his promise to tell Pharaoh about Joseph. It was easy to look forward to being released. Any day now Joseph would hear the guards as they entered the prison door to free him. Any day now.

Perhaps it was just as well that Joseph didn't know what had really happened. This way he had hope. Had he known the truth, he would have known that Berraf completely forgot about that promise. In fact, he completely forgot all about Joseph.

Berraf went about his duties as wine taster just as he had done every day before he had been in prison. Joseph, on the other hand, waited and waited—and waited some more.

20

EACH day that Joseph remained in prison seemed like forever. When Berraf was first released, Joseph couldn't wait to wake up each morning, for he felt certain that he would be set free that day. But it never happened. It had now been two long years since Berraf left.

Gradually Joseph's hopes faded and he turned his attention back to the other prisoners. They still needed him. There was no hope for them—why should Joseph be any different? Maybe God wanted him to stay right where he was. That might not be so bad. He was well fed and cared for. He had become close friends with the chief jailer and the other prisoners.

But, oh how he longed to see sunshine again! He knew that outside those heavy stone walls the seasons changed. People on the outside could look up and see stars at night. They could smell fragrant flowers in the spring. They could run, if they wanted to, just as far and as fast as their legs would carry them. These were the things Joseph missed as he sat in that prison. But he tried not to dwell on the impossible. Nothing was ever going to change. Or was it?

One day, the prisoners were dozing away the long, boring afternoon hours. Outside the door they heard excited voices. They strained to hear the conversation, but the thick walls made it difficult. Finally the heavy door opened and the chief jailer rushed into the room where the startled prisoners sat.

"It's happened! Joseph, it's finally happened!" The jailer ran immediately to where Joseph sat propped against the wall.

"What has happened?" All this excitement, and no explanation!

"Joseph, you're free!"

"What? Free?" The words were yelled by all the prisoners together.

As he struggled to unlock the thick iron cuffs, the jailer tried to explain the wonderful news. "Pharaoh himself has requested your release. You're to go to him at once. His guards will take you there. Oh, Joseph, isn't it great? You've waited so long, but now you're finally out of this place!"

Joseph's hands and feet were free from their chains for the first time in many years. He stood in the middle of the room, still dazed. Was this really happening to him? Or would he awaken to find it was a cruel dream? He stretched his arms above his head and felt the wonderful feeling of using muscles that had been still too long.

The other prisoners watched him, smiling. The joy on their faces took him by surprise. He saw no envy, no resentment. It made him suddenly sad. They had been his closest companions all these years. Now he was free. But what about them? There would be no release for them.

"Let me have just a moment with my friends," Joseph's voice was strangely quiet as he spoke to the chief jailer. The jailer needed no explanation. He left the room, and Joseph turned toward the gentle faces of the other prisoners.

"When I first came here, I was sure my life was over. I wondered if my God had forgotten me. What I didn't realize was that God was right here with me all along! Just as God will always be with you if you desire it."

Joseph felt tears rush to his eyes. "God will never forget you. Nor will I." Turning quickly from them, Joseph stepped out of the room and into the sunlight.

Pharaoh's two guards escorted him to a waiting cart. Whirring through the busy streets of the city, Joseph could hardly take in all the sights. He had missed the smells and the noise, and he wanted to drink them in all at once. Too soon they arrived at the palace.

Joseph was taken inside where several attendants guided him to the guest quarters. Without wasting a moment, a bath was drawn for him, and his dingy prison garments were tossed aside forever. Once in the marble tub, he was bathed with sweet perfumes and oils. His long, scraggly beard was shaved and his unruly hair received a much-needed trim.

"You will want to wear these garments." The tall, heavy attendant now proudly displayed a white linen tunic. Joseph ran his hands across the milky white cloth, and his thoughts were suddenly far away.

Though he stood in the very palace of the Pharaoh of Egypt, surrounded by attendants and servants, Joseph's heart was back at home in his father's tent.

There in front of him was the beautiful robe. "Try it on," Jacob was telling him. "Try it on!"

"Try it on." It was now the voice of the attendant. Joseph's mind was brought abruptly back to the present.

He put the linen tunic around him and tied it with the gold silk cords. He caught his reflection in the gleaming golden panels on the walls. The sight made him gasp. Who was this man? Joseph hadn't seen a reflection of himself in almost eight years. The face he saw belonged to a grown man, and the body no longer held the strength of a muscular, hardworking youth. Truly his years in prison had taken their toll. He looked pale, but he still held his shoulders back and his head high.

"Pharaoh will see you now."

Following three guards down the corridors and through the magnificent rooms of the palace, Joseph's mind was filled with questions. In all the fuss over his appearance, he had forgotten to ask just why the Pharaoh wanted him released. What did Pharaoh want with him? Why had he waited so long? What would happen next? Joseph took a deep breath. The heavy doors leading to Pharaoh's private chambers were just ahead now.

"God, I ask you to be with me now!" Joseph's prayer was a silent one. "You alone know what lies beyond those doors. Help me to fulfill your purpose."

The massive doors opened, and Joseph was taken inside.

21

WHEN Joseph was told he was entering Pharaoh's private chambers, he envisioned a stately throne at the end of a long, grand hall. He was surprised, then, when the doors opened into a quiet bedroom. It was a large room, but certainly not like the glorious throne room Joseph expected.

Large chairs were draped with elegant silk cloths. The tapestries on the wall reminded Joseph of those in Potiphar's home. At the far end of the room, a fire burned softly in the stone fireplace. Nearby, at a beautifully carved desk, sat Pharaoh himself.

He had been dictating to a scribe, and the two men looked up sharply when Joseph was ushered into the room. Pharaoh dismissed the scribe with a wave of his hand. Joseph was brought to Pharaoh's desk.

Again, just like the room had been, Pharaoh's appearance was almost a disappointment to Joseph. All the time he had been in Egypt, Joseph had heard about this Pharaoh yet had never actually seen him. Potiphar spoke with such great admiration about him and so did everyone else.

In Joseph's mind, Pharaoh had always been tall, and strong, and very much like a warrior. In fact, Joseph figured that Pharaoh probably wore heavy battle armor all the time. But the Pharaoh who approached Joseph now was not like that at all.

Pharaoh was—ordinary. He was not tall. His graying hair was thin and curly. He was wearing long linen robes, not battle armor. Even his manner was meek. A Pharaoh is not usually meek at all, of course. But something had happened to this one that had shaken him, even frightened him.

Pharaoh spoke directly to Joseph. "I am glad you have come. I hope that you will be able to help me." Pharaoh's voice was firm and controlled, yet Joseph sensed the uncertainty.

Realizing that he was actually in the presence of the ruler of all Egypt, Joseph dropped to one knee and bowed his head in reverence. How did one address a Pharaoh?

"I will do whatever I can, sir," Joseph's voice was humble, yet reassuring. He was relieved when Pharaoh asked him to stand.

All but two attendants were asked to leave the room, and Joseph sensed that he was about to be trusted with something private. He was deeply honored. Pharaoh directed Joseph to the chairs which were near the fire, and the two of them sat down. Joseph waited. Finally, this mighty ruler, this frightened man, began to speak.

"Joseph, I am deeply troubled. Three nights ago I had two dreams. I am upset because I don't know what they mean. When I woke, I called for all the magicians and sages of Egypt and told them about the dreams. But not one could tell me what the dreams meant. For two more days, I worried about my dreams. I was at lunch today, discussing the problem with an adviser.

"Berraf, my wine taster, was standing nearby, and overheard this conversation. He interrupted me and said the most unusual thing," Pharaoh paused and stood up. He paced nervously around the room for a moment before continuing.

"Berraf said, 'Today I remember my sin!' I didn't know what he was talking about and was about to express my irritation with him. But he went on to explain that while he and Manaded were in prison, they both had unusual dreams. He said that a Hebrew prisoner was able to interpret both of their dreams, and that everything happened just as the Hebrew said it would."

Joseph shifted uncomfortably in his chair.

"Anyway," Pharaoh went on, "I asked for your name, then had you released at once. Joseph, you must help me. I must know what my dreams mean!" Pharaoh was staring right into Joseph's eyes. On his face Joseph saw panic.

"I have never been able to interpret dreams by myself, but God will tell you what they mean. Now just exactly what were these dreams?" Joseph looked intently at Pharaoh and waited.

Pharaoh sighed deeply, as if gathering courage. "In the first dream," he began, "I was standing on the bank of the Nile River. All of a sudden, seven sleek, fat cows came right up out of the river! They walked onto the grass and started to graze there. As I watched them, seven more cows came up from the river. But these cows were skinny and bony. . . . I could see their ribs sticking out. I've never seen cows that looked so awful." He stopped.

Joseph could tell that the picture of those skinny cows was not a pleasant one for Pharaoh. Finally he went on.

"It is hard to describe what happened next. The skinny cows went over and stood near the fat ones, then—then the skinny cows *ate* the fat ones! But even after they had eaten them, the skinny cows were still skinny. Then I woke up!" Pharaoh wiped perspiration from his face.

"And the second dream?" Joseph asked.

"In the second dream, I saw seven heads of grain all on one stalk. Every kernel was perfect. Then suddenly seven more heads of grain appeared on the very same stalk. But these heads were all dried up and shriveled by the wind," Pharaoh rubbed his forehead with shaking fingers.

"Then these dried up heads of grain swallowed up the plump ones! Oh, what does it mean, Joseph?"

Joseph was quiet for a minute. "Both dreams mean the same thing."

Pharaoh looked up. "Well?"

"God has used these dreams to tell you just what God will do here in the land of Egypt."

Joseph could tell that Pharaoh was frantic with impatience, so he hurried to explain. "The seven fat cows, as well as the seven plump heads of grain, mean that there will be seven years in Egypt when everything will go well. There will be plenty of rain, and the crops will all grow better than ever before."

Pharaoh's face brightened. This was good news! Joseph saw that he was hopeful. He wished he didn't have to tell the bad news.

"But," he quickly added, "the seven skinny cows and the seven dried up grain heads mean that seven years of famine will follow. The rain will not come; all fields will wither and die. The famine will be so awful that all of the seven years of growth will be forgotten."

Pharaoh spoke almost in a whisper, "What shall we do?"

"The fact that God gave you two dreams with the same message means God wants to make sure you know that these things are certainly going to happen, and happen soon! The only chance Egypt has to survive this famine is if you store up all the grain you possibly can during the time of growth." Joseph was speaking calmly and firmly now. He knew that Pharaoh was badly shaken by what he had just heard.

"I would suggest that you find someone you can trust, who can be depended upon to handle things wisely. Put him in charge of a program to organize the farming and storing of grain."

Joseph stood, and walked as he spoke, for his head was full of ideas. "I would suggest that you divide Egypt up into five districts. Let your officials collect all the excess crops from each of those five districts. Store them in the royal storehouses. By the time the seven years of growth are over, there should be plenty of grain stored up to feed everyone during the seven years of famine.

"If you don't do this—" Joseph stopped and stared

hard at Pharaoh. "If you don't do this, disaster will strike. Your people will starve."

Pharaoh sat perfectly still for a long time. He had wanted so badly to have his dreams interpreted. Now this! Still staring blankly at the floor, he waved his hand, signaling that he was to be left alone. After Joseph and the other two attendants had left the room, he pondered the message for quite a while.

Surely Joseph was telling the truth. Pharaoh knew he was. Now his beloved Egypt would be in danger. But not in danger from other armies. That Pharaoh was equipped to fight. No, this danger was from an unseen enemy—famine. The picture in Pharaoh's troubled mind that day was a frightening one. His people, women, children, men—all with nothing to eat. Dying.

Something had to be done! The calm, businesslike suggestions from Joseph kept echoing in his mind. "Get someone wise and put him in charge," he had said. Someone wise.

As the late afternoon sunlight sent its golden shafts across the room, the fire in the stone hearth died away. Soon it would be dark in Pharaoh's room. He still sat in the same chair. "Someone wise," he said softly. He smiled to himself. He knew just exactly whom to put in charge.

Joseph.

22

A CLOUD of dust rumbled across the desert. The source of the dust was a speeding chariot, pulled by a strong black stallion. The sweat on the mighty horse's neck glistened in the midday sun, and his mane blew freely as he ran in the wind. Behind him, the chariot flew. Its wheels were nothing but a blur. Bronze plates on either side flashed in the sun. The driver sent his whip cracking through the air. Faster. Faster.

Joseph had never felt so free. He stood at the reins of the chariot and sent it flying as if he were outrunning fire itself. His cloak whipped in the wind behind him and the dry heat of the desert stung his face. He was alive with the feeling of power.

On and on he drove the horse, until the outskirts of the city demanded that he slow down. The horse coughed and wheezed in exhaustion as it trotted through the streets. Soon it would be back in the familiar stables of the palace.

Joseph stopped at last, within the walls of Pharaoh's courtyard. Immediately, several servants rushed to attend him. He stepped down from the chariot and walked toward the palace itself.

"I was afraid you weren't going to make it back at all!" A shy young boy took Joseph's cloak. "I have drawn your bath already. The feast will begin at sunset. You will have to hurry!"

"Don't worry, Jonat, I would not miss my own wedding feast!" Joseph's laugh was hearty, and he was still breathing heavily from his chariot ride. "I just wanted to clear my head for a while, that's all. I suppose that some would say that I was out for my last ride of real freedom." He smiled at young Jonat as they walked upstairs to Joseph's room.

"Perhaps you prefer your freedom to being married to such a beautiful woman?" Jonat teased his master, for he knew how Joseph had waited for this day to come.

"She is beautiful, isn't she?" Joseph had a faraway look in his eyes. "I never dreamed that one day I would really be a married man."

Jonat left his master alone to bathe. As Joseph lowered his dusty body into the tub, his thoughts carried him back to his first days in Pharaoh's court.

Because of his wisdom and character, Joseph had been appointed prime minister of all Egypt. He was in charge of the entire grain storage project. Joseph remembered fondly when Pharaoh had placed his own signet ring on Joseph's finger and put the royal golden chain around his neck.

He had said to Joseph, "You have obviously been

given strength by your God." Then Joseph had bowed down and Pharaoh had declared his authority.

For the last two years, Joseph had worked hard. The crops were growing beautifully, better than ever before. Sometimes it was difficult to remember that a famine was coming. But Joseph did remember. During the harvest seasons, he ordered that extra grain be stored; the storehouses were already getting full.

But now a new excitement had entered Joseph's life—a beautiful young girl named Asenath. Her father was a priest of the sun god Re. When Joseph first met her, he was unusually shy. She was attending a palace feast with her father, and the Pharaoh arranged for her to sit next to Joseph. He was swept away by her loveliness. She was gentle and spoke softly. But her dark eyes looked right at him when he spoke, as if she had never heard anyone speak so intelligently before. Joseph found himself thinking about her for days after the feast was over.

Eventually Pharaoh noticed that his prime minister was distracted and dreamy. He said, "Joseph, surely it is not barley that holds your thoughts captive!"

Joseph was embarrassed. "I'm sorry, sir. I do have other things on my mind."

"Yes, I think I know what you mean," Pharaoh smiled. "Things like long, dark hair and soft brown eyes?"

Joseph faced reddened. He was in love, and it showed.

Taking matters into his own hands, Pharaoh arranged for the wedding of Joseph and Asenath. It would take place in just one month, following a grand feast in the palace.

Now the wonderful day had come. As Joseph lingered in his bath for a few more minutes, he wondered about marriage. What would it be like? He thought about the people he had known. Had Annet ever really loved Potiphar the way Asenath loved Joseph?

And what about his own parents? Joseph hadn't thought about Jacob in such a long time. But he thought of him now. He remembered the way Jacob's face softened whenever he spoke about Rachel. Finally, at thirty years of age, Joseph understood how his father had felt. He wished for Jacob today. He longed for him to know Asenath. Joseph suspected that Jacob would have loved this beautiful daughter-in-law.

"It's getting late, sir," Jonat's voice cut abruptly into Joseph's thoughts.

"Alright, I'm coming." Joseph stood and reached for his soft robe. It was time to get ready. Soon he would be a married man! For a moment, the thought was scary. Then Joseph remembered the loveliness of Asenath's face, and the soft touch of her hands. Suddenly he couldn't wait.

23

ASENATH stood near the window of her bedroom. Below she could see most of the palace grounds. Servants and guards attended to their regular duties, but she paid no attention to them. She was watching for someone else. She was watching for her Joseph.

For three days he had been gone. He had left with other palace officials to travel the countryside around Egypt and see for themselves just how badly the farmlands along the Nile were suffering. Rain had not come for a long time.

Even the grounds surrounding Pharaoh's lovely palace looked dry. The lush green plants had begun to turn brown, and where grass had once grown there was now only hard, dry dirt. Out in the city, the drought's devastation was even more visible. Fewer and fewer vegetable carts lined the market square. There were no flowers, no juicy fruits for sale. Only wind and sand.

"Mother, when will Father be back? I want to show him the wooden sword I have carved!"

Asenath turned from the window. She forced a smile for her young son, Manasseh. "Any day now," she promised. But secretly even Asenath was a little worried. Where was Joseph? He had already been gone longer than he had planned.

Five-year-old Manasseh sensed that his mother was worried; he put his chubby arms around her knees. "It's alright, Mother. He'll be back soon. Until then, I'll take care of everything."

"What a brave little man!" said Asenath. "Your father will be very proud of you."

"I'm very brave, too!" Three-year-old Ephraim had come into the room and was waiting for his share of Mother's praise.

"Yes, Ephraim, you *are* very brave! How lucky I am to have two brave sons!" Asenath gathered both boys in her arms. Still, she was anxious for her husband to return. In the seven years they had been married, this was the longest they had been apart.

Later that afternoon the noise in the courtyard awoke Ephraim from his nap. He ran to his mother's room.

"He's back! Mother, Father's chariot is in the courtyard!" Ephraim's eyes were wide with excitement. "Let's go see him! Please!"

Asenath's heart beat with relief. Like her little boy, she was anxious to greet Joseph. Together they ran down the stairs and through the long hallways into the courtyard. Manasseh had already reached the chariot.

"Father!" Both boys ran to their father's waiting

arms. He lifted them high on his broad shoulders.

"Is everyone alright? Did you look after things while I was away?" Joseph spoke cheerfully to them, but Asenath saw that he looked tired and a little discouraged.

"Alright boys, there will be time to visit later. Let your father catch his breath." Asenath gently guided her two excited sons toward the house. She nodded to a servant who took them back upstairs.

"It's good to be home." Joseph greeted his wife with a soft kiss.

"Joseph, how are things? Is it as bad as they say?" Asenath's deep concern showed on her face and in her voice. Together she and Joseph walked inside.

"It's worse. Entire fields of wheat never even came up from seed. The ground is as hard as iron. Nothing will grow now, nothing but dirt."

Joseph brushed dust off of his cloak. His face was grimy from sand and sweat. "Let me have a chance to clean up, then we'll talk." He patted her hand gently, then walked toward the grand staircase.

Asenath watched him slowly climb the stairs. She saw his exhaustion and his despair.

That evening, after supper, Joseph and his wife watched the moon climb over the walls of the courtyard. As they sat on the veranda, a cool breeze blew their hair. Joseph told his wife about the effects the drought was having on the people of Egypt.

"For a while they managed to keep their crops alive." His voice was soft, but filled with emotion. "But the hot winds kept blowing, and the ground became impossible to cultivate. Now there's nothing but emptiness. No grain. No vegetables. Nothing."

"Will they be coming to get stored grain now?" Asenath remembered the years of careful planning. The royal storehouses were overflowing.

"They'll have to. Without the grain, all those people will starve," he looked grimly at his wife.

"Asenath, they are families. They have children, just like we do. Little boys that have nothing to eat! Every time I visited one of those farms and saw the little children, I could only think of Manasseh and Ephraim. I'm so frightened about this famine."

"The grain in the storehouses will feed them, Joseph. They will have plenty to eat. Don't worry." She laid her head against his strong shoulders and heard him sigh deeply.

"My God has promised to provide for them. Why is believing that promise so hard?" Joseph was tired. He got up and prepared to go inside.

Asenath got up, too, and walked with her husband.

"Joseph, all of your life your God has been faithful to you. Don't let your discouragement keep you from believing now. There will be plenty of food to eat, for everyone. Not only the people who live in the land of Egypt, but for people living miles and miles away." She squeezed his hand and together they walked upstairs to bed.

That night, Joseph lay awake long after Asenath had fallen asleep. Her words were encouraging to him, and he thought about what she had said: ". . . not only the people who live in the land of Egypt, but for people living miles and miles away. . . ."

The moon shined brightly that night. Joseph

watched it through the open window of his bedroom.

Hundreds of miles away, someone else was lying awake watching that same bright moon. The breezes were so delightfully cool that the old man wanted to sleep outside. He stretched his mat and his blankets out on the sand near his tent. He looked at the moon and tried not to let his fears overtake him.

There had been no rain for such a long time now. The sheep were growing skinny and weak. Without grass to graze on and water to drink, the whole flock would soon die. Surely there was an answer somewhere. Surely God did not intend that a whole family starve.

Jacob got up from his mat and walked in the bright moonlight to a big flat rock. Kneeling beside that rock he began to pray. He prayed for God to provide an answer. Jacob's faith was strong, and he knew that God would hear his prayer.

24

TWO days after Jacob's prayer, his oldest son, Reuben, returned from a short visit to the nearby village. He was in a hurry to get home. He had exciting news for his father.

"They say there's grain in Egypt!" He was still panting from hurrying the last mile toward home.

"What, Reuben? Slow down, you know I can't hear well."

Taking a few deep breaths, Reuben started again. "There is grain in Egypt! Apparently during the years of good growth, they were storing away excess grain. Now they say that the royal storehouses are full."

"How will that help us? We don't live in Egypt," Asher was being his usual negative self.

"The people in the village say that the Egyptian officials are willing to sell the grain to anyone who wants to buy it!" exclaimed Reuben.

"You mean we would have to travel all the way down to Egypt just to buy grain?" Simeon had just returned from a long sheep drive and was in no mood for another trip.

Jacob could contain his irritation no longer. Slamming his fist down hard on the table, he bellowed out in anger, "Why are you just standing around arguing about it? Are you so lazy that you wouldn't be willing to go to Egypt where the grain is just waiting to be bought? We could all starve to death while you complain!"

And so it was decided that all ten of the older boys would travel to Egypt. Benjamin, although almost thirty, was not allowed to go with them.

Jacob was an old man now, but the painful memories in his heart were as clear as if they had happened yesterday. Just as he had said he would, he still grieved for his beloved Joseph, whom he thought had been dead almost twenty years. Benjamin was all he had left to remind him of Rachel. There was no way he would allow Benjamin to go to Egypt.

The next morning the ten brothers were packed and ready to go. They kissed their wives and children good-bye and stood before their father. The prayer of blessing was solemn. The journey would be a long one; unless it was successful, the whole family would surely die. The women let silent tears roll down their cheeks as Jacob lifted his shaking voice to the heavens.

"Oh God, you are mighty and strong. We are frail and frightened. Lead these men, Lord, to the land of Egypt. Give them safety and health on their journey, and bring them home once again. Into your hands we place them. Amen." Jacob's white beard blew gently in the morning breeze as he kissed each son good-bye.

They traveled for days. None had been as far as Egypt before; all were nervous about the journey. They didn't know the Egyptian language, and communicating in that foreign country would be hard.

Of course Reuben, the oldest, was the leader. He carried with him some hastily scrawled maps that Jacob had drawn. He also brought a leather pouch containing money to buy the grain.

Some of the brothers clearly did not want to go along. Even though they were all grown men now, they grumbled and complained like cranky children. It was all Reuben could do to keep them from fighting among themselves. He was greatly relieved when, at last, the beautiful Egyptian city came into view.

They took a few minutes to wash their faces and change out of dusty traveling clothes before they approached the market area. Just as Joseph had been, they were overwhelmed by the sights, sounds, and smells of such a large city.

"We are here to buy grain," said Reuben to a merchant on the crowded street. "Can you tell me, please, where we need to go?"

The old man stared blankly. He did not understand a word Reuben had said. Reuben picked up a stick and drew a picture in the sand. He drew a stalk of grain and a tall grain silo. Simeon chuckled at the drawings behind his brother's back. He doubted that anyone would ever recognize what Reuben was asking.

But apparently the old man knew exactly what Reuben was asking. He pointed a stubby finger in the direction of some tall silos on the far edge of the city.

Next Reuben tried to draw a bag with coins inside.

He was anxious to find out how they were supposed to purchase their grain. But the old man was through helping. He turned his back on Reuben and walked off.

"Well," said Judah, "no one can say Egyptians aren't friendly!"

"We'd better get going, it's late." Reuben led the group of weary brothers through the narrow streets in the direction of the storehouses. As they got closer, the crowds got thicker and thicker.

"We'll never get any grain now," whined Asher. "Look at all these people! I knew this was a bad idea. We might as well go home."

"Look, Asher, we've come this far; we can't just turn around and walk all the way back. We'll stick it out. Eventually they'll get to us," Reuben tried to keep his brother calm. But even he was a little discouraged. There were just so many people!

Arriving at the storehouses, they were met by palace guards. Using translators, the guards questioned them about where they had come from and how much grain they wanted to buy. They were then sent to a make-shift "office" where their payment would be accepted.

The line waiting outside the tent which served as an office stretched half a mile. It wound between the huge silos and moved slowly. The ten brothers finally found the end of the line and began to wait their turn. It would take hours for them to reach the official's table.

As the afternoon sun dropped lower in the sky, Reuben worried that darkness would settle before they reached the table. He was afraid the line would close, and they would have wasted their time. He worried about how much they would be charged, and whether their would even be enough grain. He worried. . . .

A cloud of dust stirred the still, warm air. Everyone turned. The prime minister's chariot! Two black stallions pulled the massive bronze chariot through the crowd toward the tent. The prime minister himself was driving the chariot and pulled it abruptly to a halt. Every eye was on him as he stepped regally to the table. He spoke to the officials who were seated there for a moment, and then turned to face the crowd.

"The hour is late. The line will now close," his big voice boomed across the sea of people like a cannon. As soon as he said the word "closed," groans of frustration rolled through the crowd. They had waited so long; now this.

The prime minister held up his hand for silence. "Tomorrow at daybreak the line will open." He walked back into the shadows of the tent.

"That's just great," grumbled Simeon. "We have just wasted two long hours."

"Where are we going to stay tonight? The city streets are packed!" Asher was tired and hungry. The line closing early didn't help his mood at all.

Before anyone could answer, the brothers were interrupted by one of the palace officials. "The prime minister has asked me to escort you to the grain office," he said. Then he turned abruptly and walked toward the tent.

The brothers trotted to keep up. They shot glances at each other that said, "Why should he want to see us? We weren't even at the front of the line!"

At the door to the tent, the official stopped. "Wait."

In a moment, he stepped from the tent and announced, "The prime minister will see you now."

Inside the tent it was dim. Their eyes were accustomed to the sunshine, and it was difficult to see anything. They groped their way along to where the prime minister was seated in a stately chair up on a platform. His robes were tossed grandly behind his back, revealing a bronze breastplate gleaming around his chest.

As the ten brothers reached the prime minister's chair, they dropped to their knees, pressing their faces to the cool sand on the ground.

Speaking through an interpreter, the prime minister turned and asked them, "Where do you come from?"

Reuben answered shakily, "We come from Canaan. We have come to Egypt to buy grain."

After a long silence, the prime minister pointed a long finger at them accusingly. Again he spoke in Egyptian, "You are *spies*! You have come to Egypt to see how bad the famine really is! You are probably reporting back to enemy forces." He stared hard at them while he waited for the interpreter to translate.

"It isn't so!" Reuben was desperate. "No! We have come to buy food. My brothers and I—" He motioned to the other men who were now too frightened to look up. "My brothers and I are all honest men. We certainly aren't spies. You must believe us!"

But the prime minister's voice only boomed louder. "Liar! You are spies! Whatever country you have *really* come from just wants to find out how much Egypt has been weakened by the famine."

"Please, sir," pleaded Reuben, "let me tell you. Our father is in the land of Canaan, and our younger brother is there with him. One of our brothers is dead. There were twelve of us altogether—"

"So what?" interrupted the prime minister. "That doesn't prove a thing. I still say that you are spies!" He slammed his fist down hard on the arm of the chair.

The frightened brothers looked up in surprise. "The only way to prove your innocence is for me to test your story." He stroked his heavy black beard as he thought for a moment.

"One of you must return to Canaan, or wherever it is you come from, and bring back to me that younger brother who is still there. The rest of you will be put into prison until he is brought to me.

"If it turns out that you have been lying and that you don't even have a younger brother, then I will know you are spies. But. . . ." he paused and tightened his grip on the arms of the massive chair, ". . . I swear by the life of Pharaoh himself that you will not leave this land until your younger brother stands before me."

With that, he stood up, and stepped majestically from the platform. Within seconds, his robes had whipped through the tent, and the prime minister was clattering away on his chariot.

Two guards who had been standing nearby told the brothers to get to their feet. They were escorted through the darkening city streets to the prison.

The prime minister returned home to Pharaoh's palace. He turned his sweating stallions over to the stable attendant and trudged to his door.

All through the evening, he refused to speak. He did not eat. He sat alone on the window ledge of his bedroom, staring at the stars in the night sky. He was shaken by what had happened that day.

25

FOR three days, Joseph's older brothers remained in prison. They sat on the same cold stone floor where he had sat for so many years. They were bound in chains attached to their wrists and ankles by heavy iron cuffs. Just like Joseph, they were stunned at the events that had landed them in jail. Unfairness, accusations, no chance to defend themselves.

At the end of the third day, the big doors opened, and two palace guards entered the prison cell.

"The prime minister will see you." Their chains were removed and they went with the guards to the palace of Pharaoh.

Despite their miserable situation, the brothers were impressed with the elegance of the palace. They walked along in hushed silence, but their eyes admired the polished marble and the magnificent displays of armor and weaponry along the hallways.

As they entered Joseph's chamber, he stood with his back to them, looking out the window onto the courtyard below. He spoke without turning to face them.

Once more an interpreter stood by to translate his words to them in Hebrew. "I have had a chance to think about your story." He was careful not to look at his brothers directly. So far they had no idea who he was. For now he wanted to keep it that way.

"I have decided to give you an opportunity to prove that you are not only telling the truth, but that you can be trusted. Earlier I had requested that only one of you return to bring back your younger brother. I have reconsidered. I will now allow all of you to return—except one," Joseph paused, then added, "I will decide which one."

He rubbed his hands across his forehead before he spoke again. "The rest of you may go home with your grain. But when you get home, I want you immediately to bring your younger brother to me. It is the only way I will know you have been telling the truth. It is also the only way that the brother remaining in prison in Egypt will be freed. Talk it over and tell me your decision."

The brothers were greatly relieved that they would not all have to stay in jail. But even demanding that one of them stay seemed quite unfair.

"He has no right to hold even one of us here!" cried Gad. "We are not his slaves. He doesn't own us!"

"What good does bitterness do, Gad?" asked Levi. "We all know why we are here."

"What do you mean, 'we all know why we're here'?" Simeon was genuinely surprised at his brother's comment. "*I* have no idea why I'm here! If you know so much, be so kind as to tell the rest of us," he said sarcastically.

"I know what Levi means," said Judah. "This has happened because of what we did to Joseph."

"Judah's right," said Levi. "Don't you remember the day we threw him into that cistern? He begged us and pleaded with us. To this day, I can hear the terror in his voice—" Levi closed his eyes. "But we wouldn't listen."

"I told you not to do it," Reuben's voice was choked with emotion. "I knew it was wrong, but you wouldn't listen. Now we are all going to die. He's probably dead now and God is going to make us pay for it."

As they conversed in Hebrew, Joseph stood quietly at the window, pretending not to understand. But their words brought tears to his eyes. Quickly he left the room and ran to his own bedroom. There he fell on his bed and cried. They were really sorry for what they had done. Reuben had even said that he hadn't wanted them to do what they had done!

After Joseph cried, he felt better. He got up and washed his face before returning to the chamber. When he entered, the brothers stopped talking and looked right at him, so he quickly walked toward the window, still being careful not to face them directly.

Using the interpreter, he asked, "Have you made your decision?"

"Yes we have, sir," said Reuben. "We appreciate your generosity in letting all of us return but one. After our grain has been purchased, we will be on our way, so we can return quickly with our younger brother."

Joseph selected Simeon. "Have him bound before you take him back to prison."

The guard stepped forward and jerked Simeon's hands behind his back. As he was being led away, Reuben called out to him, "Don't worry, Simeon! We'll hurry back for you as fast as we can. I promise!" Then Simeon disappeared through the door.

"Take these men to the grain office." The meeting with the prime minister was over.

Once more the crowds at the grain office were tremendous. But this time, instead of having to wait at the end of the long line, the ten brothers were taken up to the front table immediately. The special attention delighted them.

They purchased the grain with the money Reuben had brought. It took quite a while to fill all the sacks and load them onto the donkeys. At last the long ordeal was completed, and the brothers were on their way home.

"Father will never forgive us for returning home without Simeon," said Judah. "Remember what happened when we came back without Joseph?"

"I doubt Father will grieve nearly so much over losing Simeon, or any one of us, as he did over Joseph!" Levi's remark still held some of the leftover jealousy they all had felt.

"Besides, what else were we to do?" Reuben spoke with despair. He was the oldest son and responsible for the safety of the others. He would be the one forced to tell Jacob what had happened. "We couldn't very well have fought off the whole army of the Pharaoh!"

"Reuben's right," agreed Judah. "It's best just to tell Father the truth this time. He will know we did all we could."

They had walked several hours after buying their grain and they were tired. As they neared a tiny village, Reuben suggested they stop for the night. Gad said, "Judah, you start the fire while I get grain to feed the donkeys."

Gad carefully untied one of the bulky sacks from the back of his donkey, and it fell to the ground with a thud. He turned the heavy sack upright and struggled with the knot that had been tightly wound around the top.

"There's something tangled in this leather tie." He worked with the knot some more. To his surprise, he found the soft leather pouch that had held their money.

Opening the pouch, Gad gasped. "Reuben! Come here, quick!"

"What's the matter now?" Reuben was stretched out on his blanket and clearly didn't want to be disturbed.

"Look what I found in my sack of grain. It's the money!"

"What money?"

"The money we paid for the grain! It was right here on top of the grain. Oh, Reuben, what will we do?"

Reuben and the other brothers crowded around Gad and his disastrous find. No one could imagine how the money got there.

"I *know* I saw you give that money to the official," Levi was bewildered. "Do you suppose he put it back in here?"

"Why would he do something like that? No, there must be some other explanation," said Judah.

"However it got here, one thing is for sure. We will be accused of stealing it!" Reuben rubbed his aching head. He was so tired, and now this. "Why is God doing this to us?"

They spent a restless night worrying about all that had taken place in Egypt. The next morning they were up early. For the next several days they walked toward home in silence. No one felt like talking.

Finally they began to cross their father's familiar grazing lands. But the closer they got to their home, the more they dreaded arriving. It would not be easy explaining to Jacob.

It was nearly nightfall when they saw the fires of Jacob's camp. He had heard them coming and ran happily to greet them. But as he came upon them, he stopped running, gripped by a familiar feeling that something was not right. Just as he had done almost twenty five years earlier, Jacob began to count his sons. One, two, three . . . four . . . five, six, seven, eight, nine. . . . Nine?

Reuben stepped forward and grabbed his father's frail shoulders. He knew what his father was thinking. He knew the pain he was reliving.

"Father, don't worry. Simeon is fine. He's alright," Reuben's voice was comforting and sure. "Now come to the fire and let me tell you what has happened."

26

"No!" Jacob's voice bellowed out in the still night air. "No! I won't let him go!"

"But Father, the prime minister said that if we don't bring Benjamin back with us, Simeon will never go free! You *must* let him come!" Reuben was desperate. He couldn't believe his ears. Would his own father let one son die in prison just by refusing to let another travel to Egypt?

"You listen to me, Reuben," Jacob looked hard at this oldest son. "You have caused me to lose two of my children. Joseph is dead. Now Simeon is in prison in Egypt. Yet you want to take Benjamin away from me too? Everything has gone wrong. I can't take a chance with Benjamin's life. I won't!"

"But Father. . . ." pleaded Reuben.

"No! My Joseph is dead. I can't bring him back. Benjamin is all I have left from my beloved Rachel. If anything ever happened to him, I would surely die."

It was not easy going about daily life around the

camp after that. The brothers couldn't believe their father's decision. Every time they looked at Benjamin, they felt a wave of grief wash over them like cold water. At night they dreamed of Simeon in prison. Would he stay there forever?

The terrible famine dragged on. Week after week passed without relief. No rain. Only wind and blowing sand. Despite their efforts to use the grain sparingly, it gradually disappeared. Their families needed to eat. Sheep and donkeys needed to eat. It had to happen. They began to run out of grain again.

Jacob found Judah on the nearby hillside one afternoon when the sky was red with blowing dirt. The two men shielded themselves from the stinging sand by throwing their long robes across their faces. Together they walked back to the camp and stepped into the calm of Jacob's tent.

"You are going to have to return to Egypt for more grain," he said to Judah.

"Father, I can't just stroll back into Egypt like nothing has happened. You don't know the prime minister. He was very clear that we should not return there without our brother—or we would die," Judah was unusually firm with his father. "We cannot go back unless you let Benjamin go with us!"

The wind whined and howled outside the tent. Jacob turned away from Judah and sat on his mat. He ran his wrinkled old hands through his windblown white hair. "Why did you ever tell him that you even had another brother? Didn't you see what you were getting into? Why did you want to bring such terrible suffering on me? Don't you think I've missed Simeon? Worried about him?"

"Father, the prime minister asked us specifically about our family. It never occurred to us that telling him would endanger Simeon, or Benjamin! How were we to know he was going to demand that we bring Benjamin back to Egypt with us?" Judah could see that his father was wrestling with his decision.

"I'll tell you what," Judah said, "let us take Benjamin back with us. I'll be personally responsible for him. If I don't bring him back safely, I'll bear the blame for it for the rest of my life, and you can do to me whatever you want." He waited.

"Father," he said gently to the silent Jacob, "if we don't go back to Egypt soon, we will all starve to death. And I'm not just talking about you and me, but about our wives and little ones. We can't just let them go hungry."

Jacob sighed a long, heavy sigh.

"You know, Father, we could have gone all the way to Egypt, bought more grain, retrieved Simeon, and been back by now, if you had let us go. We're running out of time."

Jacob knew that every word his wise son Judah had spoken was true. At last, reluctantly, he agreed.

The other brothers were greatly relieved. Reuben made a point of telling Judah how much they all appreciated his gentle wisdom in dealing with Jacob.

The day before they were to leave, Jacob directed Reuben and Levi to gather several sacks full of perfume, honey, spices, pistachio nuts, and almonds. These were to be given to the prime minister as a gift. Hopefully this gesture would win his favor, and he would release Simeon without further problems.

Jacob also told his sons to be sure to take *double* the amount of money they would need to buy grain. He wanted to make sure the money found in the sacks was repaid. Perhaps it had just been someone's mistake.

It was a familiar and moving scene. The nine older brothers, joined by Benjamin, stood in the early morning sunlight. The donkeys brayed their complaints about the heavy load. Little children clung to their father's knees, while older children tried to look dependable. Wives tucked small packages inside their husbands' packs at the last minute. And Jacob watched. Just before they left, he led them all in prayer.

As before, they walked the long, long distance to Egypt. The only one among them who was genuinely excited about the trip was Benjamin. For everyone else, this was a journey like many before. But for Benjamin, this was a brand new experience. He had been so sheltered and protected by his father that he had never traveled anywhere without Jacob. Though he was a fully grown man, this was his first taste of independence. He loved it!

27

THE bustling crowds of the Egyptian city were thrilling for Benjamin, but Reuben had too much on his mind to notice the merchants or the carts of vegetables. He led his brothers directly to the grain office. They ignored the long lines and walked right to the front table.

"We have come to see the prime minister," Reuben explained to the officials. "Please tell him that we have done what he asked and would like to see him." They waited for half an hour while a messenger ran to find Joseph.

At last they stood before him again inside the heavy tent at the grain office. His richly ornamented robes and shiny breastplate fascinated Benjamin. Never before had he seen such a noble man.

After hearing Reuben's comments, Joseph turned. He spoke to his attendant in Egyptian, which the brothers could not understand.

"These men will be my guests for dinner at my

home at noon. Take them to my palace and prepare a feast for them."

The attendant led the brothers away from the grain office and through the city streets to the palace grounds of the Pharaoh. Benjamin was overjoyed to be entering the grounds, but Reuben was worried.

"We are probably being taken to the palace prison. They probably know all about the money found in our sacks. Now they will accuse us of stealing. We'll be taken as slaves!"

Gripped with fear, they approached the entrance to Joseph's palace. Judah saw one of the prime minister's household officials standing in the doorway and approached him boldly. To his relief, the official quickly found an interpreter.

"Sir, you may remember that we were here in Egypt several weeks ago. At that time we purchased grain to feed our families. Well, a strange thing happened that has bothered us a lot. You see, when we were returning home, we stopped for the night and opened our grain sacks. There on top was the money we had paid for the grain! We have no idea how it got there, but we wanted to return it.

"Here, this should replace what we found in our sacks. There is also enough in this bag to pay for the additional grain we need," Judah handed the official the leather bag.

The official smiled warmly. Handing the bag back to Judah, he said, "Don't worry about it. We collected your money when you bought grain the first time. There is no need to repay us. Your God must have replaced your money for some reason."

Inside the beautiful palace, the atmosphere was relaxed. The brothers were delighted to see that Simeon had already been released and was waiting for them.

"What took you so long?" he wanted to know.

Reuben didn't have the heart to tell him that Jacob had valued Benjamin's safety more than Simeon's release.

"Never mind what took us so long. We're here and you're safe!" They hugged each other and joined their brothers, who were bathing their dusty feet in basins of cool water.

Just before noon, the prime minister entered the room. They all bowed before him. Again he carefully avoided facing them and spoke through his interpreter.

"How are your families getting along? Was the grain useful in feeding your flocks?"

They nodded pleasantly. The prime minister seemed not quite as frightening as on their first visit. Maybe the worst was over.

"And your father?" Joseph went on. "Is he still alive?"

"Yes," replied Reuben. "He is alive and well. He has sent gifts for you. We have given them to your household attendant."

Joseph turned to face Benjamin directly. He knew that Benjamin had only been a boy of ten when Joseph was sold. He felt confident that he could look at Benjamin now without being recognized. Benjamin was still resting on one knee out of respect for the prime minister. Joseph gently touched Benjamin's shoulder.

"And this must be the youngest brother that you

told me about. I am very pleased to see you. God be gracious to you."

Suddenly Joseph was overcome with his emotions. Without saying anything, he left the room quickly and ran down the hall to a quiet study. Closing the door behind him, he cried.

His own words to Benjamin, "I am very pleased to see you" echoed in his mind. *He has no idea who I am,* sobbed Joseph to himself. *I spoke to him as one absolute stranger would speak to another. Oh, but it is so good to see him again!* After a few minutes Joseph washed his face and joined his brothers for the noon feast.

The grand dining room was elaborately set for the meal. Joseph had instructed his servants to prepare a table for his eleven brothers. Now he told each where to sit. At one end of the table he placed Reuben, then Simeon, Levi, Judah and Dan. On the other side he placed Naphtali, Gad, Asher, Issachar, Zebulun, and finally Benjamin.

At first the brothers paid no attention to the seating arrangements. But Judah suddenly had a jolting thought: the prime minister had seated each according to their age in the family! How on earth could he have possibly known who was the oldest and who came next? He mentioned this to Levi, but before they could say more about it to the other brothers, the food arrived.

And what a glorious feast it was! Never had this family eaten such a splendid meal. There were exotic fruits and vegetables, spiced eggs and sweet breads, and many kinds of meats. Interestingly, the pork which Hebrew faith forbade eating was missing.

The servants had placed the food on Joseph's table. He did not sit with his brothers, for they knew that for an Egyptian to actually sit with a Hebrew for a meal was unthinkable. Joseph instructed his attendant to serve Benjamin five times more than the others. He enjoyed the looks on their faces when this was done.

"Well, Benjamin, you won't have to eat again for a whole week!" laughed Asher.

"Yes, Ben," said Simeon, "I believe the prime minister has taken a liking to you!"

The whole meal was filled with laughter. Reuben and the others were so relieved to see Simeon again. They had also been pleasantly surprised at the hospitality of the prime minister. He wasn't such a bad guy after all!

Joseph sat alone at his table and watched his brothers enjoy themselves. He could not join in their conversation, for that would reveal who he was. Instead he just watched and listened. It was so good to see Benjamin again. He had grown into a handsome young man, and Joseph was proud of him.

There was sadness in Joseph's heart, though, as he watched his family. They would soon finish their meal, buy their grain, and return to Canaan. He might never see them again. And what about his father? Just knowing that Jacob was still alive and well didn't satisfy Joseph now. He was not, he decided, quite finished with his family. He must do something, *something* to get his father to Egypt. But what?

Joseph's mind went to work. He would have to think fast. It would soon be time for the feast to end. At last he had an idea.

28

THE long afternoon was spent at the grain office. For Benjamin, the crowds were almost overwhelming. He was anxious to begin the trip home. Being away from his father this long was more difficult than he had expected.

At last the sacks were filled with grain. It was almost dark. The brothers were offered lodging near the grain office. They were told their donkeys would be loaded and ready to go at dawn.

So they spent one last night in that vast Egyptian city. They were tired of the noise and ready to get home.

The next morning, at dawn, they arrived at the office. Just as they had been promised, their donkeys were standing sleepily near the table. It took only minutes for the homesick men to start off.

Back at his palace, Joseph had spent a sleepless night. How would the plan he had set in motion the day before turn out? What the brothers didn't know was that Joseph had instructed the grain officials to secretly replace the money in the sacks again. Joseph had told them to do this once before, which was how the money bag had appeared in their sack. This time Joseph had another trick up his sleeve.

"Joseph, what is troubling you so much?" Asenath's soft hands massaged his tight shoulder muscles as he was finishing breakfast. "You have been a bundle of nerves ever since your brothers came back to Egypt. They will be on their way back home this morning. Can't you just let them go? Why are you still so upset?"

He brushed her hands aside absently and stood up. "I'm sorry I've been so moody. It's just that in all these years in Egypt, I never dared to dream I would see them all again. I had no idea it would bother me so. Now that they've stepped back into my life, I can't think of anything else. I want to see my father!"

He turned to face Asenath. "I just can't rest until I see him! Can't you see that?" He rushed from the room and left her standing alone.

"I want you to stop those men who left the grain office this morning," Joseph growled his orders to the guards who stood near the palace entrance. "When you catch them, you are to say to them, 'You have been treated well. Why, then, do you repay kindness with stealing?' "

Joseph explained what the guards would find in one of the brothers' sacks, then he barked, "Accuse them of stealing. Then bring them back to me. Now go. Quickly! They are getting away!"

Joseph went inside and closed the door behind him. He sank down into a chair and closed his eyes. Was he doing the right thing? His mind was troubled. He must talk to God.

He opened the door. "I do not want to be disturbed again until the men are brought back to me," he said to the servant outside. Then Joseph went back into his office and got down on his knees to pray.

"God, how gracious you are to allow me to see my family once more! I thank you for letting me do that. Lord, when I first saw them, they all bowed to me. It was then that I knew that my dream of so long ago had been fulfilled. In that dream, their stalks of grain had actually bowed down to mine.

"With all that has happened in my life, I sometimes wondered if you had forgotten about that dream. Forgive me, God, for ever doubting that you would make it come true," Joseph paused and rubbed the back of his aching neck.

"And now, Lord," he went on, "they will be coming back to me, and I will tell them who I am. Please give me wisdom and courage for that moment. And God, I ask you to allow me, your servant, to see my father just once more. I know you are a gracious God. Amen."

Just outside the city, horses rumbled across the desert plains. They kicked up dust and dirt that could be seen for miles.

"What is that?" Reuben had glanced back over his shoulder and caught a glimpse of the thundering cloud approaching them.

"I don't know, but it looks like they're heading right for us!" Simeon was uneasy. His stay in prison had done nothing to help his nerves.

"Let's stop. They can't possibly want to hurt us." So

Reuben and his brothers sat down to await whatever was coming.

"Hold it right there! All of you!" The guard jumped off of his horse and yelled at the surprised brothers. "You are ordered to stay right where you are!"

"What's the problem?" asked Reuben.

The officer repeated the accusation from Joseph, just as he had been instructed to do. "You were treated well. Why, then, did you repay the kindness of the prime minister by stealing his royal drinking cup?" The officer glared at Reuben.

"What?" Reuben couldn't believe what he was hearing. Perhaps he had just misunderstood the man.

"I am saying that the royal drinking cup is missing. The prime minister has reason to believe that you have stolen it," said the officer.

"You don't know what you're talking about! We aren't thieves! What kind of people do you think we are?" Judah was frantic.

Reuben spoke more calmly. "Look, you are welcome to search us. Yes, I know that last time our money accidentally ended up back in our sacks, but we didn't steal it then—and we didn't steal anything now!"

Reuben stood eye to eye with the officer now. "Go ahead and search us," he said confidently. "If you find the prime minister's silver cup in someone's sack, let that brother die. And the rest of us will be slaves to the prime minister for the rest of our lives."

"Yes," the others agreed. "Search us. We have nothing to hide!"

"I will do just that," replied the officer, "but if I find the cup in one of your sacks, that one must return with me to be a slave. The rest of you will be allowed to go free."

He turned to the other guards who had dismounted and were standing quietly beside their horses. "Search them!"

Starting with Reuben's donkey, every sack was untied and removed, opened and searched. As more and more brothers were pronounced innocent, they began to relax.

At last the guard came to Benjamin's donkey. By this time all the brothers were joking about having to load up all over again.

What the brothers didn't know, of course, was that Joseph's trap was about to spring. Joseph had received a beautiful silver drinking cup as a wedding gift from a grateful Berraf. Joseph treasured the cup and used it every day. The day before his brothers left Egypt, he told his attendant to see that the cup was hidden in Benjamin's grain sack. This had been done at night as the donkeys were loaded.

The trap snapped shut. The guard quietly said, "Well, and what have we here?" His hands had been buried up to the wrists in grain, but they now brought out something that flashed brightly in the morning sun. A silver cup!

29

DID you think that I was such a fool," said Joseph to his bewildered and frightened brothers standing before him, "that I would not notice that my silver cup had been stolen?"

Reuben spoke first. Through the interpreter he said, "Sir, you would not believe us if we told you that we were innocent, and I cannot blame you."

He stopped and groped for more words. "God is punishing us for a sin that we committed long ago. A sin which has nothing to do with you. But we must now accept that punishment. We have all returned here to you so that not only Benjamin will have to serve as a slave. All of us are willing to be slaves."

"No!" Joseph's voice boomed through the huge hall. "Only the one in whose sack my cup was found will be allowed to stay. The rest of you are *ordered* to return home."

Judah could stand it no longer. The impact of what was about to happen stabbed at him. He stepped forward and faced the prime minister without fear. "Sir, let me just speak honestly to you. If you are a compassionate man, you will at least give me this chance to tell you what is on my heart."

He waited. When the prime minister said nothing, Judah gathered his courage to continue. "On our first trip to Egypt, you asked us about our father. At that time we told you about him and this younger brother. We also told you about our other brother, who we said was dead.

"That brother, and Benjamin here, are the only two sons my father had with his wife, Rachel. He loved Rachel so much, just as he loved those two sons. It was hard for us to understand sometimes. It even seemed to us like he hardly loved us at all."

Joseph's eyes were fixed steadily on Judah, but inside his heart was melting.

"Anyway, we did something terrible to our brother and we told our father he was dead. We never told him the truth about what we did. Believing his son was dead just about killed our father. The only thing that has kept him going since then is his love for Benjamin. That's why it was so difficult for us when you demanded that we return without him to Egypt!

"Don't you see? If we go back home without him now, our father surely will die! He told me so when we left, and I know it's true!"

Joseph felt the tears stinging the back of his eyes, but he did not break down. He clenched his teeth tightly to bottle up all the emotion welling up inside.

Judah went on. "I told my father that I would be responsible for Benjamin—and I meant it. Now if you have decided that Benjamin is guilty, I cannot change that. But I ask you, I *beg* you to allow me to take his punishment. Let him return home to my father. I will stay and be your slave," Judah's voice had not wavered. His head was held high and his shoulders were erect. Never before had Joseph been so moved by the courage of another man.

Turning to his attendants, guards, and servants, he shouted, "Out, everyone out! I wish to be alone with these men." It did not take long for the dutiful men to obey their master's command. In a moment the door was closed and the room was hushed.

Joseph stood near the window. How would he tell them? What would he say? He turned and looked at them a minute before he said anything. Speaking in Hebrew now for the first time he quietly noted, "I think the thing I've missed most is Leah's barley-fig bread—"

Simeon gasped. But no one spoke. They were too confused. Here was the prime minister of all Egypt standing before them, speaking in Hebrew about their mother's barley-fig bread.

Joseph waited a moment, then spoke again. "I have always wondered just when Asben found out we had used his well," Joseph was starting to have fun with them now.

Their faces were still blank.

He threw out another clue. "When you first heard that dream about your stalks of grain, and how they would one day bow down to mine, did you ever have any *idea* it would come true?"

"Joseph?" said Benjamin softly. He was probably the

only one of Joseph's brothers who had been the least bit interested in that dream.

"Yes, Benjamin, I am Joseph," his voice was amazingly quiet.

"Joseph!" Reuben's deep voice roared with excitement. Suddenly no one was quiet any more. "Joseph, Joseph! I can't believe it's really you!" Everyone was shouting now and rushing forward to hug him.

This was the moment he had only dreamed about for so many years. He was overwhelmed by their tears and joy in knowing he was alive.

"Tell us what happened! How on earth did you end up here?" Simeon wanted the whole story.

When they had begun to calm down, Joseph motioned for them to join him on cushions piled on the rugs in front of the fireplace. He rang a bell, and a servant entered the room. The servant was surprised to see the prime minister of Egypt sprawled on the floor in the middle of all these men, laughing and hugging them still.

"Bring us refreshments!" Joseph told the servant. "We have a lot to catch up on!"

They talked for hours. First Joseph told them everything that had happened to him, from the day they had pulled him up out of the well to the day he first saw his brothers in Egypt.

There were times, during his recounting, that the things he told them made them uneasy. He sensed their discomfort when he talked about being unjustly accused by Potiphar's wife. He knew it was unpleasant for them to listen to his stories of being in prison. Their guilt deepened with each new story of Joseph's woes.

Joseph knew this. Finally he came to the very heart of what was troubling them. "Don't be angry with yourselves. Don't blame yourselves. God had a purpose in everything. God needed me here in Egypt. Had I not been where I am now, you might not have been able to get grain. The whole family might have starved. Don't you see? The first step in getting me to Egypt was throwing me into that cistern!"

They talked into the night. "The famine will certainly last another five years," he told them. "It will become harder and harder for you to get food. God has made me prime minister of all Egypt. Bring your families and flocks and stay here until the famine is over. It's the only way you will survive."

But there was another reason Joseph wanted them all to move to Egypt. He was desperate to see his father. He told his brothers the same thing he had told Asenath. "I will not rest until I see him again."

"But here!" Joseph slapped his knee and jumped up. "We have talked all night. I know you'll be leaving soon, but there's someone I want you to meet first." He rang the bell and a servant entered the room.

"Tell my wife that we will have guests for breakfast! She will know what I mean," Joseph waved his hand and the servant left quickly.

In a few minutes Joseph and his brothers were noisily making their way to the private dining hall. They stopped as they came into the room.

There before them stood a beautiful Egyptian woman. Her dark hair was braided with golden strips of linen, and her white robes showed off her delicate figure. Standing on either side of her were two small boys.

The older one had dark hair like his mother, but his eyes were piercing like his father's. The younger boy yawned and let his round face lean on his mother's robe. His light brown hair was curly, but he had his mother's beautiful round eyes and upturned nose.

Joseph called to the little boys, and they rushed into his waiting arms. "Sons, I want you to meet some special people. These are your uncles!" The boys turned to face the smiling men.

"These are my sons, Manasseh, and Ephraim." There was pride in Joseph's voice.

Asenath came over and stood quietly beside him. She placed her hand gently on his arm.

"And this," Joseph turned to face her, "is my wife, Asenath."

"If they are really my uncles, why haven't I seen them before?" Manasseh was overwhelmed by this family reunion. His question was answered with good-natured laughter from Joseph's brothers.

Reuben picked Manasseh up and placed him on his broad shoulders. "That's a long, long story," he said. "And I'm not sure I want to be around when your father tells it to you!"

"Mother, will they be staying with us forever?" asked Ephraim.

Before Asenath could answer, Benjamin stepped forward. He had been standing quietly in the back of the group. Taking little Ephraim into his arms he spoke gently, "Ephraim, now that we are finally all together, we will never be apart again. But first we need to go back to Canaan and get our families. Did you know you have many cousins you haven't met?"

Joseph smiled at the beautiful picture before him. He had never dreamed that his youngest son would be sharing this moment with Benjamin. Joseph hoped it would be the first of many such moments.

And so they prepared to return to Canaan. Joseph helped them get ready. He provided them with wagons to carry all the grain. The wagons would also be useful when they brought their wives and children back to live in Egypt. The brothers were wearing new clothes that Joseph had given them, and they were anxious to show Jacob the gifts that Joseph was sending along for him.

To Benjamin Joseph gave five changes of clothes and three hundred pieces of silver. Joseph couldn't seem to do enough for his little brother. He had a special word for him as he left. "Bring him here to me," he told Benjamin. "Bring Father to Egypt."

They all hugged and tried not to be too weepy. "Don't quarrel along the way!" Joseph shouted to them. Their laughter rang through the air.

Joseph watched them leave. He stood on the grand balcony of the palace with Asenath and waved as they disappeared into the city. His heart was almost at peace, for he had been reunited with his brothers.

But he was also worried. He was so close . . . so close to seeing his father again. Now he wondered. Would Jacob live through the difficult journey? Would he live long enough to see Joseph once more?

Joseph and Asenath walked inside together. There was nothing to do now but wait. He would just have to wait. And pray.

30

JACOB sat under a lonely cedar tree on the desolate hillside. Never in his long life had he felt so miserable. He had missed all his sons, but he especially missed Benjamin. *I was a fool to let him go,* he grumbled to himself. *I'll never see them again, any of them.* And so he sat under that tree, counting his troubles.

In the distance he heard a noise. Could it be? *No, Jacob, you're an old man. You're imagining things.* Still the noise grew louder. It had to be his sons!

Jacob struggled to bring his brittle legs to a standing position. Shielding his eyes from the sun with his hand, he searched the horizon. They must be coming from that direction. Would they never appear?

At last he saw a caravan in the distance. As it drew closer, his heart sank. This caravan had wagons, lots of them, and far more donkeys than his sons had taken to Egypt. No, this wasn't his family. It was just a big caravan crossing the desert.

Still he watched, for he was interested in who they might be, and where they were going.

"Father!" Was someone calling him?

"Father, we're home!"

Benjamin? Could that be Benjamin's voice coming from that strange caravan?

"Don't you know us? Your traveling sons have returned!" Benjamin had broken away from the others and was running toward his startled father.

Never had Jacob been so happy to see anyone. He grabbed his youngest son and held on as if he never wanted to let him go again.

"Father, listen." Benjamin pulled away from Jacob's embrace so he could look into his face. "Father, Joseph is alive!"

The old man just stared at Benjamin. He worried that either he was so old he was hearing things, or Benjamin had gotten too much sun. But Benjamin repeated it.

"Joseph is alive. I saw him myself!"

"I don't know what you're talking about," Jacob frowned at him. "Is this some kind of cruel joke you are playing on an old man?"

"No, Father. It's true! You must believe me. See the wagons? They are filled with gifts from Joseph. You can ask the others!"

As they spoke, Reuben and Simeon walked up and greeted their father warmly. Simeon was especially glad to see him, and hugged him tightly.

"Has he told you?" asked Reuben. "About Joseph?"

"I think you're all crazy. I don't want to hear his name used to make a fool of me!" Jacob was starting to get angry. They knew how he felt. Why were they deliberately trying to hurt him?

"Father, I know it's hard to believe, but he *is* alive," Reuben put his big strong hands on Jacob's shoulders. "Now come back to the camp with us. We'll sit down and tell you all about it. You won't believe it!"

At first, they were afraid Jacob *wouldn't* believe it. But it was hard even for Jacob to come up with an explanation for the wagons and clothes and gifts.

Finally he allowed his heart to risk even more incredible pain. He allowed himself to believe. Joseph was alive. His beautiful, precious Joseph—alive!

The story was a painful one for Jacob to hear. He learned for the first time about the lies of his older sons, and about their hatred of Joseph. He learned about Joseph's difficult life in Egypt and felt the pain of his son as only a father can. At last their story ended. It was late and they were tired. They wanted to spend time with their wives and children.

Jacob was left alone. For a long time he sat by the fire that night. Then he quietly got up and went into his tent. When he came out, he carried an old cloth wrapped around something. The cloth was brittle with age, and Jacob carried it gently and carefully, like a newborn baby. He left the warmth of the fire and walked silently up the hillside.

The ground was bathed in brilliant moonlight. Jacob reached a plot of loose dirt and slowly got down on his knees. For a few minutes he dug in the soft earth with his hands, until he had a small hole about a foot deep. He unwrapped the cloth bundle, and delicately removed its contents. There in his shaking old hands he held the tattered, bloody remains of Joseph's beautiful coat.

Placing the coat in the hole, he lovingly covered it with dirt. Then he bowed his gray head. "God, you knew all along. You knew what your plan for Joseph would be. *I* wanted him to carry the birthright. *I* wanted him to be greater than his brothers. But I never really stopped to ask what you wanted for him.

"I see now that this coat is a symbol of everything that I wanted for Joseph. I'm going to bury it here, and I'm never going to look at it again. But someday, God, let me look at my Joseph again. . . ."

The next day, Jacob's family packed up all their tents and belongings and left for Egypt. It was a long and difficult trip. Traveling with an old man, small children, and flocks of sheep and goats was slow. But Jacob was strong. His desire to see Joseph kept him going. He would make it. He just had to.

One night on the journey Jacob felt the very presence of God. In his heart Jacob knew that God would bless him and his family. God spoke to him that night, and reassured him of things to come. The next day would be the happiest of Jacob's long life.

Early in the morning, Jacob sent Judah ahead into the land where they were to settle.

"Tell them we will arrive late today."

Judah left and quickly made his way into the city. He headed straight for Joseph's palace and told him the good news.

Together, Judah and Joseph jumped into a chariot and raced for Goshen. Never before had Judah ridden in a chariot, and the experience was a thrilling one! Joseph drove the horses faster and faster, until Judah felt like they were about to leave the ground!

The chariot ride seemed an eternity to Joseph. Would they never get there? Were these horses just standing still?

Then they came over a gentle hilltop, and the land of Goshen lay before them. The flocks and wagons had already arrived. There were animals and children everywhere. Joseph searched the crowd that was now his own family, but he couldn't see Jacob anywhere. His heart was beating wildly. Where was his father?

Reuben came out of a small lean-to that had been hastily set up near an old well. He came to Joseph and greeted him warmly.

"Where's Father? Is he alright?" Joseph asked impatiently.

"He's fine, Joseph. It was hot and we wanted to get him out of the sun, that's all. He's resting. I'm sure when he feels a little stronger, he'll want to see you—" But Reuben's words were interrupted.

From deep inside the shadowy lean-to a frail but familiar voice said, "Is that my Joseph I hear?"

At the sound of that voice Joseph's hands shook violently. He could hardly catch his breath.

An old man stepped forward from the shadows into the bright sunlight. His white beard and hair blew gently in the breeze, and he groped for something to steady him. "Is that Joseph's voice I hear?"

"Yes, Father, it is." Suddenly Joseph was like a timid little boy. He waited for just another moment, then a giant sob shook him from head to foot. "Oh, Father!" He rushed forward and threw his arms around the frail little man who swayed unsteadily near the tent.

"Joseph. . . ." Jacob could say no more. He just held his son and wept.

The other brothers stood by awkwardly. They felt like intruders, but they were unable to tear themselves away. So they just silently watched.

Jacob lifted his head and looked Joseph squarely in the eye. "God has answered many prayers for me today," he said. "Now I am ready to die, for God has allowed me to see you once more."

Joseph smiled gently at his father. "No, Father, I've waited too long to see you. Don't go and die now! Besides, you have two grandsons you haven't even met."

Jacob slowly shook his head and smiled. "Two more grandsons!" He looked around him. Over sixty members of his family were gathered there. "Two more grandsons. . . ."

But deep in his heart, Jacob somehow felt that they would be the most special grandsons in the whole world.

The Author

Lee Ann Lewis grew up in Midland, Texas. She and her husband, Marc, moved to Dallas with their two children, Lauren and Jason, in 1981.

Pursuing her interest in drawing, Lee Ann created a comic strip, "Sparky," for her children's elementary school newspaper. She has conducted a cartooning seminar for students at a Young Author's Conference, and taught art classes to first-graders in an East Dallas housing project.

Lee Ann is a graduate of Bible Study Fellowship, and she and Marc serve as sponsors for the "I Have a Dream" Foundation. They are members of Wilshire Baptist Church in Dallas.

In addition to writing and drawing, Lee Ann enjoys quilting, baking, skiing, and travel.